GHOST STORIES

STORIES

A Saga Magazine Collection

GHOST STORIES

A Saga Magazine Collection

Saga   **P**
PROFILE BOOKS

First published in Great Britain in 2014 by
Profile Books Ltd
3A Exmouth House
Pine Street
Exmouth Market
London ECIR OJH
www.profilebooks.com

10 9 8 7 6 5 4 3 2 1

A CIP catalogue record for this book is available from the British Library.

ISBN: 978 1 78125 372 4
eISBN: 978 1 78283 118 1

Text design by *sue@lambledesign.demon.co.uk*
Typeset in Garamond by MacGuru Ltd *info@macguru.org.uk*

Printed and bound in Great Britain by
CPI Group (UK) Ltd, Croydon CRO 4YY

CONTENTS

INTRODUCTION

PERVERSELY, THERE'S SOMETHING COSY about a good ghost story. Linked as they surely are to the winter festivals of Hallowe'en and Christmas, the anticipatory thrill of reading a tale of dread makes drawing around a crackling fire – darkness swirling outside – that much more enticing.

So this collection, I hope, will both warm and chill in equal measures. It opens with the vintage 'A Vignette' by M. R. James, the acknowledged master of the ghost story. The fifteen stories that follow his classic tale are the result of a competition run by *Saga Magazine*, which (as any fule kno) is *the* magazine to read if you are both smart and over 50. Literary, too – the magazine's talented readers sent in more than 1,000 entries to our competition, an astounding response and surely an indication of a vast resource of untapped talent out there. As one of the judges, I was amazed at the sheer quality of the writing that poured out from pens and keyboards across Britain. Congratulations to our winner Mal Howard for 'Homecoming', and runners-up Alan Wright for 'Crying in the Attic' and Margaret Cramb for 'Beyond Butcher's Broom'.

Ghost stories are as old as sputtering tallow candles and creaking wooden steps. Ever since their earliest days in spoken folkloric form, unworldly beings have stalked the page, the stage and latterly the screen, right up to the present day. Witness Shakespeare's poor Banquo and Scrooge's stalker, through to Susan Hill's *The Woman in Black* and countless films and TV programmes today. But it wasn't until Victorian times that ghost stories emerged as something of a genre, fuelled by a craze for gothic novels and a cache of horror stories emanating like ectoplasm from Germany.

Perhaps the most famous exponent of the art of the ghost story was M. R. James, a medievalist scholar who from 1904 to the late 1920s cornered the market in ghoulish tales of the supernatural. His storytelling usually included a characterful setting, a 'normal' and perhaps naive person as protagonist, and the discovery of an old book or other antiquarian object that somehow unlocks the unwelcome attention of a super-natural menace.

More than 100 years on, it is remarkable how many entries to our competition still echo this structure, and how well it still works. The innocent start, the promising setting, the strange discovery, the creeping feeling that something is horribly wrong and finally the chilling denouement are all used to remarkably skilful effect here.

There were a few other striking things about our cache of stories. One was the number of writers (including Mal

Howard, our eventual winner) who used the railways as their setting. From abandoned platforms to doors that shut just at the wrong time, one can only guess at the harm that long-term exposure to Britain's railways has done to these writer's minds. The family home was another recurring motif: the very place that should represent safety and sanctuary does just the opposite, with threat in the wainscot, appalling secrets in the cupboard under the stairs and malevolence in the attic.

Though writing techniques may have remained similar down the generations, ghost stories themselves do seem to have evolved, both in this collection and in the arts at large. There seems to be a drift away from the bloodthirsty and evil – today's ghosts are growing subtler and more poignant, and ghost stories can even introduce us to spirits that are benevolently inclined. Alice Sebold's *The Lovely Bones* is one example, the film *The Sixth Sense* is another, and there are a few in these pages too.

Why should this be? In an age of increasing non-belief, are we are still searching for hope that there is life after death – and a kind, benign one at that? Which of us really wants to believe that departed loved ones have gone for ever or that, after we ourselves have gone, we will not be able to have some control over whatever unfinished business we have left behind?

I leave the thought with you. But benign, even funny, though some of the spirits in the following pages may be, if a sleepless night is really what you are after, don't worry

– they are counterbalanced by a comforting number of eerie, fiendish ghouls.

So turn off the lights, stoke the fire, light a candle – hey, pour a whisky too! – and thrill to these wonderful tales, woven from the clever minds of some of our dear, wonderful readers of *Saga Magazine*.

Katy Bravery
Editor, *Saga Magazine*
August 2014

A VIGNETTE

M. R. James

YOU ARE ASKED TO THINK of the spacious garden of a country rectory, adjacent to a park of many acres, and separated therefrom by a belt of trees of some age which we knew as the Plantation. It is but about thirty or forty yards broad. A close gate of split oak leads to it from the path encircling the garden, and when you enter it from that side you put your hand through a square hole cut in it and lift the hook to pass along to the iron gate which admits to the park from the Plantation. It has further to be added that from some windows of the rectory, which stands on a somewhat lower level than the Plantation, parts of the path leading thereto, and the oak gate itself can be seen. Some of the trees, Scotch firs and others, which form a backing and a surrounding, are of considerable size, but there is nothing that diffuses a mysterious gloom or imparts a sinister flavour – nothing of melancholy or funereal associations. The place is well clad, and there are secret nooks and retreats among the bushes, but there is neither offensive bleakness nor oppressive darkness. It is, indeed, a matter for some surprise when one thinks it over, that any cause for misgivings of a nervous sort has attached itself to so normal and cheerful a spot, the more so, since neither our childish mind when we lived there nor the more inquisitive years that came later ever nosed out any legend or reminiscence of old or recent unhappy things.

Yet to me they came, even to me, leading an exceptionally happy wholesome existence, and guarded – not strictly but as carefully as was any way necessary – from uncanny fancies and fear. Not that such guarding avails to close up all gates. I should be puzzled to fix the date at which any sort of misgiving about the Plantation gate first visited me. Possibly it was in the years just before I went to school, possibly on one later summer afternoon of which I have a faint memory, when I was coming back after solitary roaming in the park, or, as I bethink me, from tea at the Hall: anyhow, alone, and I fell in with one of the villagers also homeward bound just as I was about to turn off the road on to the track leading to the Plantation. We broke off our talk with 'good nights', and when I looked back at him after a minute or so I was just a little surprised to see him standing still and looking after me. But no remark passed, and on I went. By the time I was within the iron gate and outside the park, dusk had undoubtedly come on; but there was no lack yet of light, and I could not account to myself for the questionings which certainly did rise as to the presence of anyone else among the trees, questionings to which I could not very certainly say 'No', nor, I was glad to feel, 'Yes', because if there were anyone they could not well have any business there. To be sure, it is difficult, in anything like a grove, to be quite certain that nobody is making a screen out of a tree trunk and keeping it between you and him as he moves round it and you walk on. All I can say is that if such an one was there he was no neighbour or acquaintance of mine, and there was some indication about him of being cloaked or hooded. But I think I may have moved at a rather quicker pace than before, and have been particular about shutting the gate. I think, too, that after that evening something of what Hamlet calls a 'gain-giving' may have been present in my mind when I thought of the Plantation; I do seem to remember looking out of a window which gave in that direction, and questioning whether there was or was not any appearance of a moving form among the trees. If I did, and perhaps I did, hint a suspicion to the nurse the only answer to it will have been 'the hidea of such a thing!' and an injunction to make haste and get into my bed.

Whether it was on that night or a later one that I seem to see myself again in the small hours gazing out of the window across moonlit grass and hoping I was mistaken in fancying any movement in that half-hidden corner of the garden, I cannot now be sure. But it was certainly within a short while that I began to be visited by dreams which I would much rather not have had – which, in fact, I came to dread acutely; and the point round which they centred was the Plantation gate.

As years go on it but seldom happens that a dream is disturbing. Awkward it may be, as when, while I am drying myself after a bath, I open the bedroom door and step out on to a populous railway platform and have to invent rapid and flimsy excuses for the deplorable deshabille. But such a vision is not alarming, though it may make one despair of ever holding up one's head again. But in the times of which I am thinking, it did happen, not often, but oftener than I liked, that the moment a dream set in I knew that it was going to turn out ill, and that there was nothing I could do to keep it on cheerful lines.

Ellis the gardener might be wholesomely employed with rake and spade as I watched at the window; other familiar figures might pass and repass on harmless errands; but I was not deceived. I could see that the time was coming when the gardener and the rest would be gathering up their properties and setting off on paths that led homeward or into some safe outer world, and the garden would be left – to itself, shall we say, or to denizens who did not desire quite ordinary company and were only waiting for the word 'all clear' to slip into their posts of vantage.

Now, too, was the moment near when the surroundings began to take on a threatening look; that the sunlight lost power and a quality of light replaced it which, though I did not know it at the time, my memory years after told me was the lifeless pallor of an eclipse. The effect of all this was to intensify the foreboding that had begun to possess me, and to make me look anxiously about, dreading that in some quarter my fear would take a visible shape. I had not much doubt which way to look. Surely behind those bushes, among those trees, there was motion, yes, and surely – and more quickly than seemed possible – there was motion, not now among the trees, but on the very path towards the house. I was still at the window, and before I could adjust myself to the new fear there came the impression of a tread on the stairs and a hand on the door. That was as far as the dream got, at first; and for me it was far enough. I had no notion what would have been the next development, more than that it was bound to be horrifying.

That is enough in all conscience about the beginning of my dreams. A beginning it was only, for something like it came again and again; how often I can't tell, but often enough to give me an acute distaste for being left alone in that region of the garden. I came to fancy that I could see in the behaviour of the village people whose work took them that way an anxiety to be past a certain point, and moreover a welcoming of company as they approached that corner of the park. But on this it will not do to lay overmuch stress, for, as I have said, I could never glean any kind of story bound up with the place.

However, the strong probability that there had been one once I cannot deny.

I must not by the way give the impression that the whole of the Plantation was haunted ground. There were trees there most admirably devised for climbing and reading in; there was a wall, along the top of which you could walk for many hundred yards and reach a frequented road, passing farmyard and familiar houses; and once in the park, which had its own delights of wood and water, you were well out of range of anything suspicious – or, if that is too much to say, of anything that suggested the Plantation gate.

But I am reminded, as I look on these pages, that so far we have had only preamble, and that there is very little in the way of actual incident to come, and that the criticism attributed to the devil when he sheared the sow is like to be justified. What, after all, was the outcome of the dreams to which without saying a word about them I was liable during a good space of time? Well, it presents itself to me thus. One afternoon – the day being neither overcast nor threatening – I was at my window in the upper floor of the house. All the family were out. From some obscure shelf in a disused room I had worried out a book, not very recondite: it was, in fact, a bound volume of a magazine in which were contained parts of a novel. I know now what novel it was, but I did not then, and a sentence struck and arrested me. Someone was walking at dusk up a solitary lane by an old mansion in Ireland, and being a man of imagination he was suddenly forcibly impressed by what he calls 'the aerial image of the old house, with its peculiar malign, scared and skulking aspect' peering out of the shade of its neglected old trees. The words were quite enough to set my own fancy on a bleak track. Inevitably I looked and looked with apprehension, to the Plantation gate. As was but right it was shut, and nobody was upon the path that led to it or from it. But as I said a while ago, there was in it a square hole giving access to the fastening; and through that hole, I could see – and it struck like a blow on the diaphragm – something white or partly white. Now this I could not bear, and with an access of something like courage – only it was more like desperation, like determining that I must know the worst – I did steal down and, quite uselessly, of course, taking cover behind bushes as I went, I made progress until I was within range of the gate and the hole. Things were, alas! worse than I had feared; through that hole a face was looking my way. It was not monstrous, not pale, fleshless, spectral. Malevolent I thought and think it was; at any rate the eyes were large and open and fixed. It was pink and, I thought, hot, and just above the eyes the border of a white linen drapery hung down from the brows.

There is something horrifying in the sight of a face looking at one out of a frame as this did; more particularly if its gaze is unmistakably fixed upon you. Nor does it make the matter any better if the expression gives no clue to what is to come next. I said just now that I took this face to be malevolent, and so I did, but not in regard of any positive dislike or fierceness which it expressed. It was, indeed, quite without emotion: I was only conscious that I could see the whites of the eyes all round the pupil, and that, we know, has a glamour of madness about it. The immovable face was enough for me. I fled, but at what I thought must be a safe distance inside my own precincts I could not but halt and look back. There was no white thing framed in the hole of the gate, but there was a draped form shambling away among the trees.

Do not press me with questions as to how I bore myself when it became necessary to face my family again. That I was upset by something I had seen must have been pretty clear, but I am very sure that I fought off all attempts to describe it. Why I make a lame effort to do it now I cannot very well explain: it undoubtedly has had some formidable power of clinging through many years to my imagination. I feel that even now I should be circumspect in passing that Plantation gate; and every now and again the query haunts me: Are there here and there sequestered places which some curious creatures still frequent, whom once on a time anybody could see and speak to as they went about on their daily occasions, whereas now only at rare intervals in a series of years does one cross their paths and become aware of them; and perhaps that is just as well for the peace of mind of simple people.

HOMECOMING

Mal Howard

THERE USED TO BE A STRETCH OF LINE that runs from
God's Forgot to Somewhere Else. That's what the wags called
it when I was a boy. Course, it's been shut down for dickey's
years, but in them days it crept slow and easy through the
Norfolk poppyfields, picking up and setting down at places
I doubt you've ever heard of: Penny Row, Becket's Row,
Ringbow, Thornham, Arby, Milby …

Little old villages, years behind the times.

I shan't ever forget that bit of line. Dad was signalman at
Arby, and we lived in a cottage right beside the box. It was
just a two up, two down, and before I got too big and had to
sleep on the sofa me and my sister Dolly used to get up in the
middle of the night and sit by our bedroom window listening
to the nightingales. I like to come down to the old station

and remember how it were before the war come and changed everything. Like tonight. There's a hint of snow in the air and Christmas 1912 eases into my mind. I was portering on Penny Row station then, fourteen years old and full enough of my own importance to fill the shiny braided cap and brass-buttoned waistcoat twice over. All the nobs from London come down that year to spend the holiday at the big house, and the tips I got you wouldn't believe.

But it didn't last. The war come and as soon as I was old enough I joined up with my mates. Left Mum and Dad, Dolly and Nellie, my girl. It was the thing to do, you see. That's how I found myself on the Somme in October 1916 with Piggy Dawson and Freddie Parsons. There had been more of us, but Billy Walker, Pat Parmenter, the Miller twins, and Captain Dalrymple from the big house were all gone. I knew it wouldn't happen to me, though, despite what Piggy used to say.

'Don't you kid yourself, Jackie boy. You en't never going home. You're going to stay here with me.'

Well, I did go home, course I did. But not poor old Piggy – or Freddie neither. That morning we was on stand-to when the Hun barrage opened up, a shell landed smack on top of our trench, and Piggy and Freddie went west. Me, I was lucky. I reckon I caught a Blighty one and lost my memory because the next thing I recall I was standing on Walsham station waiting for the Arby connection. There were plenty like me in them days, drifting about with no clear recollection of what they was doing or why or even who they were. At least I knew that much; I was Jack Felmingham, eighteen years old and going home to see my girl.

When the train pulled in I made for a carriage up front, empty save for two farmers sitting opposite each other in the far window seats and too deep in conversation to notice me.

The guard's whistle had gone when the door was flung open and a fat, perspiring man in a tight blue suit thrust two wicker baskets on to the floor and hurried in after them.

'That was a near 'un,' he announced to no one in particular and heaved the baskets on to the rack. He sat down, rubbing his hands together with a dry, sandpapery sound. 'Christ, it's cold in 'ere.' He looked towards the two farmers. 'Don't you think it's cold in 'ere?'

They ignored him and he sat back with a grunt, opening up a *News Chronicle*.

'It's a bit on the chilly side,' I said, friendly-like. He slowly lowered the paper and looked through me, then resumed his reading. I caught sight of the headlines:

NEW OFFENSIVE ON SOMME. HEAVY ENEMY LOSSES

'Heavy enemy losses,' I thought bitterly, and Piggy and all the others was in my mind. 'What about our bloody losses?' I looked above the paper to the fat man who, oblivious to my gaze, continued to suck his teeth and read the racing results. I hated him for that, for his blindness in not seeing the thousands dying on the front page.

The train slowed, stopping at Penny Row, and I heard the porter shouting. Curious to know who had taken my place, I craned my neck and saw him, thumbs in waistcoat, all important.

'Not 'alf as smart as I was,' I thought. Then I looked down at my dirty, stained uniform and dark buttons. 'But a bloody sight smarter than I am now.'

I sank back in my seat. The door opened and a young woman, pretty she was, flustered and spilling packages, struggled in. In her haste she almost sat on my lap, then sprang up, shying away like a startled hen.

'Sorry, Miss,' I said. ''Ere, let me help you.' But she coloured up, retrieved her packages, and sat in the middle of the seat opposite.

I kept staring at her from under my cap. She reminded me of Nellie in a way, dark hair, hazel eyes, but thinner.

'Skinny,' Ma would have called her; 'No work in her.' That's why Ma and Nellie got on so well. Nellie was a great worker.

I must have embarrassed her with all that staring, for she wouldn't look in my direction but kept her head turned away. Either that, or fat blue suit's cigarette smoke was annoying her. So I looked at the pictures above the seats. I particularly liked the one in the middle: Brixham Harbour, it was, and that made me think of Aunt Flo. She went there one year. Smelt like Yarmouth, she said, all fishy. But she liked it. I ought to go and see her, poor old dear. She lived out Briston way – I could borrow Dad's bike, be there and back in an afternoon.

Funny how one thought leads to another. Thinking about Flo reminded me of my last day of leave. She had come over to tea, and afterwards me, Dad and Uncle Charlie her husband had popped down to the Flying Horse for a farewell drink. Charlie had been a regular in the Norfolks and served in Africa during the Boer War.

'You watch them buggers, Jackie,' he kept saying. 'Pop your 'ead up and they'll have yer.'

'We en't fighting the Boers, Charlie,' Dad said. 'It's the Germans.'

'Boers, Germans, what's the difference?' demanded Charlie.

He was right, of course. Don't matter who's on the opposite side, a bullet kills you just as quick.

I come to as the train slowed for Becket's Row. No one got off or got on. It were always afternoon in Becket's Row, dozing away in the middle of nowhere. Even their pub was a private house with a trestle table and a couple of barrels. We waited there while they dropped off chicken crates and things, and I watched a two-horse plough harrowing for winter wheat. For a moment I envied the man his sure and unchanging purpose in life. But I tossed the thought aside for the railway was in my blood, same as Dad and Grandad before me. After the war, who knew what the future held? Head porter, guard, stationmaster, not just at Arby or Milby, but Walsham or even Norwich. And then me and Nellie would be settled as we always dreamed we would.

The train jerked into motion again, and fat blue suit, who had been dozing, came to and stared about with uncomprehending eyes. He settled back with a gusty sigh and slept again.

I watched the pink pantile roofs fall behind as we took the Low Dyke curve, making for the Ringbow straight. Nearly home, and I felt the joy of it knot my stomach as I thought of Mum and Dad, Dolly and Nellie waiting for me. I worried a little because I couldn't remember whether I'd let them know I was coming. But it didn't matter much; I knew they would be there.

At Ringbow the two farmers parted company. 'Fare ye well, old partner,' the tall one said. 'See ye in Norwich Sat'day.' The door slammed and he was gone, his place taken by a cadaverous clergyman who disapproved of all he saw. His lowering gaze rested momentarily on each of us: contempt for blue suit; appraisal for the girl with the downcast eyes; a challenge for the farmer, who stared back insolently, and for me uncertainty as if he were unsure of my right to be there. I fixed my eyes on Brixham Harbour again. That place where Aunt

Flo stayed – ideal for a honeymoon. Why not? Perhaps not a week, but a couple of nights maybe. That'd be something, wouldn't it? More than Mum and Dad ever had. A day on Yarmouth beach, that's all they got.

They were lighting the oil lamps on Thornham station as we screeched to a stop. Fat blue suit struggled to life and heaved his baskets from the rack.

'Thornham, is it?' he demanded, bending to read the station sign.

'That's right, Thornham,' I replied.

He struggled out of the carriage and stood on the platform blowing on his hands. The young woman got off too, and I was glad to see a young man come forward to take charge of her parcels. Then we were off once more, trundling the last few miles to Milby. In the compartment no one spoke or moved. Perhaps the farmer and clergyman slept, I don't know. I sat with my eyes closed until I felt the quickening pace as we slipped down the gradient into Arby and I knew I was home.

Old Billy Postal the porter was on the gate and I called out to him over the heads of the passengers.

'Hello, Billy,' I said. 'How's Doris?'

He was too busy collecting tickets to hear me. But his old cross-bred collie did, though, and came slowly forward, head down and growling in his throat.

'What's up with you then, you silly old bugger,' I said. 'You know me, don't you?'

He backed away, belly down and whining. I'd never seen him act that way before, and neither had Billy. He left the gate and came over.

'I don't know what's got into him, Billy,' I said.

He ignored me, bending down to grab Sam's collar.

'Shut that row, you silly great fule,' he ordered. 'There en't nuthin' there.'

Sadly I walked up to the little house. The curtains had not yet been drawn and I watched for a while. Their faces lapped by lamp glow, they bent over their chores, Ma, Dolly and Nellie. I didn't go in – didn't seem much point. Piggy was right after all. Perhaps we both were.

THE CRYING IN THE ATTIC

Alan Wright

THERE IS A COMMON MISCONCEPTION among the general populace concerning the nature of haunted houses. Lurid legends abound in relation to castles and grand old mansions, where strange hauntings, headless horsemen and ladies dressed in white (or grey, as the ectoplasmic fashion dictates) are frequently documented.

Yet it has been my experience, as an investigator for the Society for Psychical Research since 1884, that the most common setting for genuine manifestations is found not in the crumbling towers of the landed gentry, but rather the humble and ordinary abode of the common man, with nothing to set the place apart from thousands of other dwellings in Great Britain.

But even here, where one would expect gruff common sense

to prevail, ghostly visitations are often attributed to family members who have passed on, but who are yet unwilling to pass over. It is a reluctance to let go that is felt by the living as well as the dead, in the way that we seek out pipe smoke to remind us of a late, beloved father.

But consider the possibility that some ghosts do not spring from the shadows of death at all. Nor from the shadow world of imminent death, as I have personally witnessed in cases of crisis apparition, where the subject is unexpectedly visited by a relative or friend, often at night, only to discover later that the visitor had, in fact, died that very moment many miles away.

I have been witness to many strange and inexplicable phenomena. I have also seen decent people duped by char-latans. I, and my colleagues in the Society, approach all circumstances with an open mind. We are cynical believers, if you will. Our objectives are clear: to consider whatever we encounter in a spirit of exact and unimpassioned inquiry, without prejudice or prepossession of any kind.

Yet the case I describe here has profoundly disturbed me, for I have never met its like before and never wish to again. The only explanation I can offer transcends religion itself. But perhaps you can judge for yourselves, even offer an alternative explanation for what happened in Lacock village.

I was first invited to the beautiful village of Lacock, in

Wiltshire, in 1893, just over a year ago. The house, close to the Abbey, was owned by a retired chemist (let us refer to him as Mr C.). He lived there with his son Ned and daughter-in-law Jane who, it must be averred from the outset, were childless.

I had received a letter from Mr C., in which he gave an account of a strange presence in his house – he refused to call it a 'ghost', being a man of scientific background and uncomfortable with anything spiritual. However, the presence was so powerful and, to him, inexplicable, that he decided to write to us, having heard that the Society for Psychical Research pursues its investigations on scientific, not superstitious, grounds.

According to Mr C., on several nights a week, the distinct sound of a baby crying could be heard from the attic. He had, of course, searched the place and found nothing remotely connected with an infant presence either now or in the past – no discarded cots or rattles or any of the paraphernalia one would expect if a baby had once lived there. That isn't to say a child had never lived there – or died there. The house was old and life and death play their part in the atmosphere of a place just as surely as furniture or photographs.

But he was at a loss to explain why this particular sound should be heard *now*. His family had lived in the house for several generations. No tales of infant mortality had ever reached his ears.

What could be the cause of this sudden manifestation?

What intrigued me, however, was his description of the baby's cries

'They're heart-wrenchingly high-pitched, Mr Byers,' he told me once I had sat down with all three of them in that delightfully cosy front room. 'Screams of such intensity, lasting no more than ten seconds, followed by short gasping sobs that again last for a very short time. Then, nothing.'

'Why say that?' Jane said with something akin to anger in her voice. 'There are the other things.'

She sat by the hearth, and I saw her face dramatically illuminated by the dancing flames of the log fire. I realised at once that she appeared to be the one most deeply affected by the sounds, and I reflected how that might naturally be the case. She was childless, after all. And because she was young, and pretty, I assumed her childlessness wasn't something she welcomed.

Her husband Ned, who was standing beside her armchair with one hand on her shoulder, spoke for the first time.

'What Jane means, Mr Byers, is … there's something else. Each of us has suffered.'

'Suffered?' I asked.

They all looked at each other.

'Coincidence,' said Mr C., but his comment lacked conviction. Then he himself took up the tale. 'There are headaches when we stand in that place. Not just the usual. They are agonising pains in the head.'

'And the burning sensations,' Jane added. 'In our arms and legs. It's as if we are on fire *from within.*'

All three looked at me searchingly. I could tell they were in earnest.

'There are cases of collective illusion,' I began, 'where several people experience the same symptoms.'

Although Mr C. nodded, I could see from the others' expressions what they thought about that.

'There's also an overwhelming sensation of agony in the attic whenever the sound is heard,' Jane said. 'As if an insidious and pestilential fog has somehow slithered its way through the tiny locked window. We cannot see it, cannot feel it. But it fills us, Mr Byers. It *possesses* us.'

The wind moaned in the chimney breast, and the flames bowed and dispersed as flecks of soot dropped on to the glowing logs.

We then turned to more practical matters. I was invited to stay for several nights so that I, too, could experience the melancholy sounds and the cloying miasma of pain and grief that had so disturbed the household. I then set about asking what I considered were delicate but obvious questions.

Ned and Jane had been married for two years and it may be that they had suffered an infant bereavement, or perhaps Jane had endured the grief of miscarriage? But no, they assured me there hadn't been any such occurrence. I thought I detected a pallor of regret on Jane's face, and it became clear to me over the next few days that she and her husband would dearly love to be blessed with child. So, too, I gathered, would Mr C., whose wife had died from consumption several years ago.

My second question followed an equal thread of logic: did any of the neighbours have a child? Sound can travel in unexpected directions, especially if the attic area is one shared with other houses in the row. The answer was an unequivocal no. Besides, Mr C. argued, how could that explain the painful aura that filled the attic room after each occurrence?

'The imagination is a powerful conjurer of emotions,' I replied.

It was on my third night there that I was woken in the early hours.

At first I thought it was a cat on the rooftops in some distress, but as my mind cleared and focused, it became obvious that the sound was that of a baby screaming intermittently. It wasn't a whimpering or a crying, not the natural sounds all babies make when they are hungry or uncomfortable. No. This was *screaming* of a dreadful intensity. And the awful sounds seemed to emanate from directly above my head.

No sooner had I dressed than I heard a knock on my door, and all three of the occupants were standing on the narrow landing outside my bedroom. Mr C. had already carried upstairs a short ladder for the purpose of climbing into the attic, and I must admit it was with some trepidation that I agreed to investigate with the aid of an oil lamp, again thoughtfully provided by my host. The three of them remained on the landing, and I caught sight of the glimmer of the lamp as it shone in the upturned eyes of the daughter-in-law. She was plainly terrified.

Once I had attained the attic, I placed the oil lamp on the floor and gazed around. It was a small, cramped area, with mouldy lumps of sacking, a small box filled with dust-wreathed storage bottles which had once contained all manner of oils and compounds, and a damaged bench balance with rusted scales, evident tools of the retired apothecary's trade.

Admittedly, the place was damnably cold, and although that is a sign suggestive of a ghostly presence, it is also an indication of poor construction and gap-filled rafters, some of which I discovered. Surely the overwhelming atmosphere of pain might be nothing more than the chill of a winter's night?

And in similar vein, perhaps the sound itself *had* been a cat, sneaking through the narrow rupture in the roof and making its nightly protests? But as soon as I pondered the idea I rejected it. A baby's screams of such agony as I heard could never be attributed to the nocturnal mewlings of a tom.

Then, with an alarming suddenness, I began to feel it: a tremendous pressure against my temples, an agonising force emanating not from some external source but from *within my own head.* My eyes began to swell so violently that at any moment I was sure my sockets would tear apart, and I felt as though my skull was about to explode.

I clamped my hands to my head and, when I tried to stumble back to the ladder, I felt a fierce heat rage through my arms and legs. I felt at any moment my blood would literally boil and my veins erupt. It was with some effort that I finally reached the ladder, where hands reached up to guide me down to the landing. Once I was there, the cranial pressure and the burning vanished as quickly as they had come.

'You felt it?' asked Mr C. almost triumphantly.

'Perhaps the wind slicing through the rafters …' I stammered. Ned added simply, 'There is no wind, sir.'

'Or I was influenced by the details you gave me …'

I let my voice fade into disbelief.

'Are you sure there is no record within the family of an infant suffering great agony before … the end?' I asked, clutching at a straw I had already clutched at.

Mr C. sighed. 'I know of no such thing,' he said.

'But it's possible?' I insisted.

'It's possible,' he said.

The following night the screams came again. Dreadful, agony-racked torments that filled one with pity for the poor suffering child. But again, despite my growing terror, I investigated and found nothing but the cold and the overwhelming and debilitating sensation of pain and grief.

And that was where we left it, an investigation with an unsatisfactory conclusion, and I set off from Lacock feeling that somehow I had failed them, offering not even the slimmest of explanations, just the promise that I would seek out advice from my colleagues. But no one could offer anything I hadn't already thought of and discarded, and so there it was left. An apologetic letter to Lacock ending with my futile good wishes.

Not the Society's finest hour.

However, a few weeks ago, almost a year to the day since my fruitless visit, I received a short telegram from Mr C. It said puzzlingly, *Please come. We have answers. We have questions.*

With my interest recaptured, I returned to the village of Lacock.

I was met by Ned, whose eyes were dark-rimmed and heavy, and yet there seemed a brightness, a sparkle in his eyes that reminded me of the way the oil lamp's flame had glimmered in his wife Jane's eyes a year earlier. Sitting in the front room were his father, Mr C., and a man I didn't recognise.

'This is Doctor Mallory,' said Mr C.

As we shook hands I looked around for his daughter-in-law. She was nowhere to be seen.

I had a cold sensation in my stomach and asked the fearful question.

'Where is Jane?'

Both Mr C. and the doctor raised their eyes heavenwards.

'I am so terribly sorry,' I stammered. 'You have my condolences.'

At which point both men began to smile, then laugh out loud.

'My dear sir!' my host exclaimed. 'My son's bedroom isn't as bad as all that!'

Later, over a celebratory brandy, I was informed that Jane and Ned had been blessed and almost cursed within the space of two months: a beautiful baby girl had become a most welcome addition to the family, but their joy was to be – it was feared literally – short-lived.

Mr C. told me how the infant had become seriously ill and began to scream with an intensity that was truly terrible to hear. He immediately thought of the phenomenon of a year ago and was convinced the sounds were exactly the same.

'You see, Mr Byers, we knew with a deep certainty what the baby was enduring, *because we had already endured it.* The pains in the head, the burning in the arms and legs. Babies cry, but they have no way of communicating to us *why* they are crying. The symptoms that cause them such agony. But we *knew*. The child had earlier developed an inflammatory infection of the skin, but that could have been caused by any number of conditions. But when I set that alongside the other symptoms we had all experienced so vividly a year ago, I recognised at once what the cause was. That dreadful disease erysipelas, or St Anthony's Fire.'

His voice was low at this point, and I heard from above the gentle lilt of a mother's lullaby.

'Doctor Mallory then acted with laudable speed once the diagnosis was so unconventionally confirmed. He applied a solution of lunar caustic to arrest the disease, followed by many hours of remedial measures which were unimaginably painful for the poor little thing.'

Later, as we gazed down on mother and baby, both sleeping, both blissfully content, Mr C. said quietly, 'A hardy spirit, my granddaughter, is she not?'

'Indeed!'

He sighed and touched my arm. 'I am a man of science, Mr Byers, yet this … With all of your vast experience in such things, how can you explain this?'

I shook my head and smiled. There were dizzying thoughts in my head, but I remained, on the surface at least, nonplussed by the phenomenon.

'There are more things in heaven and earth than are dreamt of in our philosophy,' I quoted in a show of levity.

'Well, perhaps the cries were a sort of forewarning,' Mr C. offered. 'The child's spirit, sending us a warning of what she was about to suffer. Sharing her symptoms with us so that we would be able to recognise them and act accordingly.'

He gave a self-conscious smile, an acknowledgement of fancy from his scientific self.

'As good an explanation as any,' I concurred.

We then parted amicably. He shook my hand with grand-fatherly vigour, and I set off for London.

On the train I had time to bring my thoughts together. He was right, I told myself, to a point.

But one thing puzzled me. And it went to the very heart of those unfathomable questions of life, death and the afterlife that worry at us all.

We suppose the spirit – the *soul* – continues to exist after death. That's what we are familiar with, a belief common to many religions, even if we don't understand it. And the soul exists, of course, during life, and even in the womb as soon as life is created. *But Mr C.'s grandchild wasn't even conceived a year ago.* Which begs the question: what if the soul exists *before conception itself*?

I laughed at the suggestion, looking at my reflection in the compartment window and the twilight world of the passing countryside beyond my ghostly image smiling back. The idea of a soul without a body, swimming around like a fish in a pond waiting for the hook!

And yet it was the only explanation I could think of.

I have been involved in many baffling cases during my time with the Society, but never one as disturbing as this. For it throws into confusion everything we believe about Life and Death and the Creation of the Spirit.

But perhaps I am being too reflective after all. Perhaps a baby's cries where no baby existed were simply a telepathic hallucination brought on by the desperate longing to conceive that I saw in Jane's eyes. Her longing, let us suggest, was powerful enough to create the illusion of a new-born child, and that illusion transferred itself to us. The agonies we heard and felt were no more than a manifestation of the bitterness she felt in being unable – up till then – to conceive. If people have powers of telekinesis, where they can cause objects to fly around the room, why not have the ability to send emotions also?

That was how I concluded my report to the Society. But it is a most unsatisfactory explanation, is it not?

Arnold Byers
Society for Psychical Research
November 1894

BEYOND BUTCHER'S BROOM

Margaret Cramb

YOU DON'T EXPECT your whole world-view to be turned upside down in the space of a few hours. As a scientist, I have never felt the need for a religion nor any belief in an afterlife. Indeed, my parents, having named me Thomas, began to call me 'Doubting Thomas' at the age of five. Reason rules my thinking. Dickens's Mr Gradgrind put my view succinctly: 'Facts alone are wanted in life.' Yet, if I'm honest, I realise that for the past couple of weeks I have been disregarding the facts, trying to find logical explanations for phenomena which have no logic. It was the sound of breathing that should have alerted me and the glimpses of movement out of the corner of my eye.

Let me go back.

Curiously for a county so rich in wild flowers, a book has yet to be published detailing all the plants of Aldershire. Montague-Paine made the first attempt to produce a flora in the 1870s – he was one of the founders of the Aldershire Society for Natural Science which established the Aldershire Museum. As well as his country home, he owned an eighteenth-century end-of-terrace house in a back street about five minutes' walk from the museum and it was there that he preserved his plant specimens, mounted and catalogued them. Some men have a shed in which to escape the nagging tongue of an unhappy wife; Montague-Paine had his herbarium room. In those days, plants were preserved in mercuric chloride, an extremely hazardous pesticide, which could be fatal if swallowed. Unfortunately, Montague-Paine was in the habit of licking the brush holding the chemical before applying it to the dried plant, with the result that he died before completing his flora. (It was a hideous death apparently – gradual corrosion of the mouth and stomach, burning pain, tremors and damage to the nervous system, leading eventually to collapse and kidney failure.) He bequeathed his herbarium and the house containing it to the museum.

In the 1950s, a fellow called Hunter had a stab at producing a flora, but he died of a heart attack in the museum herbarium as he was approaching the end of the task and his draft mysteriously disappeared. Now it is my turn. I have remained a bachelor, live alone and, having taken early retirement from teaching, I can devote all my time to the work. I am fortunate in having access to the notes prepared by Montague-Paine, as well as up-to-date botanical records.

Montague-Paine was, by all accounts, a solitary, curmudgeonly, competitive fellow who refused requests from other eminent Aldershire botanists to join him in creating the flora. Well, I can understand that. Appleby wanted to join me in producing this one, but I prefer the sound of *Bell's Flora of Aldershire* to *Bell & Appleby's Flora of Aldershire* (or, worse, *Appleby & Bell's*).

Besides, I haven't forgiven him yet for claiming the record for a new ten-kilometre square for the nationally scarce Little Robin (*Geranium purpureum*), knowing full well that I had told him it was there.

⇥•⇤ ⇥•⇤

We haven't seen much of the sun this October. At dusk yesterday the sulphur yellow sky beyond purplish-grey clouds suggested gales and storms to come. My flat is on the first floor of a large Victorian house in a tree-lined road on the outskirts of town, within walking distance of the museum. This morning I walked through scurrying autumn leaves in strengthening winds under a darkening sky, but the anticipated rain had not yet arrived.

As usual I collected the keys to the herbarium room and house from the museum before it opened to the public – the

front door is unlocked by staff and I can tap in a code to enter
the inner door. Having obtained the keys, I went out on to the
High Street through the huge front doors of the mock-medi-
eval (actually late Victorian) building, turned right and then
right again into the dark narrow covered alleyway between
two shops, leading to the quiet back street which Montague-
Paine knew so well. It is like walking into a different world,
away from the bustle of the High Street. For some reason, I
felt surprisingly depressed and reluctant to proceed. By rights,
I should have been feeling buoyant: today I would be final-
ising Butcher's Broom (*Ruscus aculeatus*) – a strange plant
with bright red berries and spiny-tipped 'leaves' which are
actually stems – and was well through the lily family, with
just the orchids still to do to complete my flora. The signifi-
cance to me was that Montague-Paine had got no further than
Butcher's Broom when preparing his flora, and I would be
covering new ground.

A further right turn at the end of the alleyway and a walk
past four other houses in the terrace brought me to my destination and my sense of foreboding increased. Taking the keys
from my pocket, the thought suddenly struck me that I had
forgotten to sign them out in the keys book at the museum.
Damn! Should I go back? I decided not to bother – apart from
myself, only Mrs Hawkins normally comes to the house on
Fridays to catalogue a collection of moths and butterflies, and
I know she is on holiday. Nobody had seen me take them and,

with luck, no one would be aware of their absence. I turned the first key in the lock and entered the side passage leading down to the garden at the rear, overgrown with brambles and nettles among the buddleia, which seemed to be fighting to get into the windows of the building. I felt the first few heavy drops of rain as the dark clouds started to disgorge their contents.

The second key opened the back door and triggered the insistent high-pitched sound of the burglar alarm. Hurriedly, I tapped in the code to silence the beast and stepped into the gloom. The cleaners have refused for years to service the house – they claim it is 'spooky' – and it has become the domain of the cellar spiders (*Pholcus phalangioides*), their tiny bodies and long legs suspended in a tangled mass of untidy webs, bearing no resemblance to the works of art of their garden cousins. I took a deep breath before opening the door ahead of me, trying to avoid breathing in the overwhelming and unhealthy fumes of naphthalene (moth balls). The room bears homage to the taxidermist's art and I hurried through the unblinking eyes of wild cats, falcons and other dead creatures preserved for ever in a semblance of life. Through the door at the other end, I breathed again and descended the dusty stairs to the basement.

I read again the prominent notice attached to the door to my left at the bottom of the stairs:

Aldershire Museum Herbarium

BEWARE

Old herbarium sheets are often preserved with
Mercuric Chloride.
Use gloves.
Wash hands thoroughly after working here.
Do not eat, drink or smoke in this area.

I unlocked the door, entered and closed it behind me. The intense cold hit me like a body blow and I began shivering involuntarily and breathing shallowly. It was always cold in here (the heating has not worked for years), but not this cold. I found the light switch and turned to look at the oil portrait of Montague-Paine on the same wall as the door. The penetrating grey-green eyes always strike me first, today seeming to stare at me with a freezing hostility. Appleby has always said Montague-Paine looks like me, but I can't see it. He reminds me of Gladstone in middle age, hair thinning on top, untidy mutton-chop whiskers framing his face and thin, wide mouth turned down at the sides.

As usual, I placed my watch on a chest of drawers beneath the portrait to avoid dust contamination, sat down at the desk facing the opposite wall and set out my papers in front of me. Although I tried to push it from my mind, my heart was sinking in the expectation of the breathing. It had started a couple of weeks ago, faint at first, gradually becoming heavier and more rasping. There it was, behind me! – apparently emanating from the portrait. Each time I turned towards it, it stopped abruptly, but I glimpsed movement out of the corner of my eye. Since I do not – did not – believe in ghosts, I put the phenomenon down to working too hard. It must have been some sort of hallucination based on my own breathing and perhaps exacerbated by the chemicals in here. I steadied myself, realising that the solution was to complete my flora as soon as possible and take a well earned break.

Still shaking with cold, I picked up the key to the walk-in herbarium cupboard to my left, where Montague-Paine's boxes of dried specimens are stored. I opened the door leaving the key in the lock and switched on the single unshaded light bulb. I walked straight to the box containing Butcher's Broom, then spun round, startled. The cupboard door behind me had slammed shut and I heard the sound of the key turning in the lock.

How many hours have I been in here? I have tried everything I can think of to get out. I've shouted until I am hoarse, my voice buried in this subterranean hellhole and drowned by the sound of beating rain, indistinct down here but no doubt loud above ground. I've hurled myself against the door repeatedly, but whatever remains of Montague-Paine has moved the extremely sturdy and heavy chest of drawers across it.

(Who would have thought there could be so much physical power in what is presumably an insubstantial being? It brings to mind the invisible hurricane-force winds I lived through twenty years ago, uprooting great beech trees and snapping huge branches.) I've called out to my tormentor, saying that I am willing to abandon my flora if he will let me out (a lie, of course, as I expect he knows – it means too much to me to let it go now). The chances of my being found in the near future are slim. No one will miss me at home, no one works in this building over the weekend and no one knows I am here as I forgot to sign out the keys. I am sitting uncomfortably on the floor, leaning against boxes of specimens on the shelves. My pen was in my jacket pocket and in here I have found some paper, albeit old and used on one side, on which to write this account of my predicament. The hope that I am communicating somehow with other human beings helps me to cling on to my sanity and stave off mental disintegration. This is far worse than being trapped alone. I sense the company of a malevolent force, determined that I will get no further with my flora than he did with his: a spirit composed almost entirely of jealousy, covetousness, hate and proprietorial desires.

I long for this torment and terror to end. My heart is pumping anxiety round my trembling body. I am trying to breathe deeply to quell my rising fear but the air seems foul and somehow unsatisfying. My saliva has dried up, my stomach has the sharp pain of emptiness. I can still hear the heavy breathing, but now it seems to be closer to me, overlapping my body and mingling with my own breath. Oh God, the

    light has

        gone out.

THE LAIRD

Anne Rogers

I'D NEVER BELIEVED IN GHOSTS. As far as I was concerned once you were dead that was it, end of story; which made it all the more surprising when I saw a woman in a long dress walk through a wall.

We were staying with friends who had recently moved to an old house in Scotland. They had been on holiday and seen this beautiful house by the River Deveron going for a song. They fell in love with it and bought it. Richard and I were both keen to visit. Richard was attracted by the fishing. I was curious. We'd finished dinner on our first evening when I distinctly saw a well-dressed woman, possibly late nineteenth-century costume, walk through a wall. The conversation around the table continued as though nothing had happened. I was obviously the only one who had seen her. I hadn't been drinking, well just a couple of glasses of wine and a small brandy; certainly not enough to account for me seeing ghosts.

I didn't say anything. Frankly, if I'd just moved into a house I wouldn't thank anyone for telling me they'd seen a ghost. Richard, I knew, would find the whole thing hilarious and I'd never hear the end of it. I almost convinced myself I'd imagined it but I knew I hadn't.

The next morning I examined the alcove where the woman had disappeared.

'Looking for something?'

The man's voice, coming from immediately behind me, gave me such a start I let out a scream and spun round. The man standing there was Hector the caretaker/odd job man we'd met on our arrival and who was due to take Richard and Brian fishing.

'I was wondering if this could have been a door at some time,' I said.

'Oh aye. It was the last folks who had it closed off. It used to lead into the servants' quarters, where the kitchen is now.'

This information did nothing to settle my nerves.

At this point the men arrived and the three of them went off fishing. I sank into a chair and wished we weren't staying until the weekend.

After lunch Celia and I walked into the hills behind the house. Looking down at it, I asked her what she knew of its history.

'Very little, really. The oldest parts are seventeenth-century, but bits have been added here and there. It's been empty for most of the last century, since the old lady died.'

'The old lady?' I queried.

'Yes. She was the last full-time occupant. Her husband, the Laird, had died quite some time before her, in "violent circumstances", I believe.' Celia grinned at me. I attempted to arrange my face into some kind of appropriate response. I felt increasingly uneasy.

'Anyway,' she continued, 'members of her family used it for holidays, fishing, and so on up until the 1980s, but it stood empty after that, until the last people bought it, and they didn't stay long.'

'Do you know why they left?' I asked

'Just didn't settle, I think. All the better for us, as they practically gave it away, and they'd had a load of work done to improve it before they moved in. If you want to know more, ask Hector. His family has been involved with the house for generations.'

I agreed to do that, although I felt that I already had more information than I wanted.

As we ate dinner that evening Richard and Brian were regaling us with tales of the 'ones that got away' when Richard suddenly said, 'Who was that?' His chair was facing the slightly open door into the hallway.

'There's no one else here,' Celia said.

'Must be the Laird!' Brian said, and they both burst out laughing. He explained that some of the locals had told them that the house was haunted by the ghost of the last Laird. 'The poor fellow had gone crazy,' Brian told us, 'and had attempted to murder his wife. She'd been saved by the servants, but in the struggle the Laird met his end.'

'Only the Laird?' I asked, my voice sounding as shaky as I felt.

'What – killed?' asked Brian.

'No, doing the haunting.'

Brian and Celia collapsed into fits of laughter.

'Gosh, Jen, one ghost's enough!' Celia gasped. This was followed by further laughter. I joined in as best I could.

As Richard and I got ready for bed I asked him what made him think he'd seen someone.

'Oh, it was just some shadows. There was obviously no one there.' Feeling it was worth the risk, I told him what I'd seen on the first evening.

'Crikey old girl, you'd better start taking more water with it!'

'You're right,' I laughed, 'must be the whisky.' As I thought, I was on my own.

The next morning, I found Hector outside chopping wood. After some general questions about the house I asked him whether it was haunted. He shot me a quizzical look.

'Some folks say the Laird haunts the house, but I've never seen him.'

'His wife doesn't join him then?' I tried to sound casual.

'She died peacefully in her bed. Why should she leave her grave?'

Good question, I thought, as I smiled and wandered away.

The day passed pleasantly enough. I was just relieved that it was our last day and, more importantly, our last night. Dinner went without incident. Celia had put on a magnificent spread for our 'last supper', as she put it. Richard overindulged as usual. His stomach was already complaining by the time we got to bed. We spent a few restless hours until he sat up and reached out to the bedside table for his indigestion tablets.

'Damn! I must have left them in the kitchen. Would you be an angel and get them for me, and a glass of water?'

He turned on his most pathetic expression. I wasn't keen, as you can imagine, but Richard didn't look well. Telling myself not to be stupid, there was nothing to be afraid of, I'm an intelligent adult, etc, etc, I made my way gingerly downstairs, turning on every light I could find as I went. I didn't care who, among the living, I disturbed. I paused outside the kitchen door and listened. Nothing. Taking a deep breath, I opened the door and switched on the light.

I've had nightmares where I've been in mortal danger and needed to scream to summon help, but when I opened my mouth no sound came out. This time it happened for real. Seated at the kitchen table was a man who looked very like Hector, wearing rough working clothes, and on his knee the well-dressed lady I'd seen a few nights before. She glanced at me, her face expressionless, stood up, turned and walked through the wall into the dining room. The man also stood up and walked directly towards me. He stopped in front of me and stared into my eyes.

Apparently my heart gave out at that point. I have no recollection of what happened next. I imagine that Richard must have eventually wondered where I'd got to and come looking for me. I feel a little bit sorry for him, but he should have gone to fetch his own tablets. I don't suppose he'll get anyone else to look after him now. Not at his age and with that paunch. Anyway, I woke up after a few days, probably after the funeral; goodness knows where I'm buried. I've been having great fun ever since. Flora and Hamish are tremendous company. Flora was the last Laird's wife and was having a passionate affair with the factor, Hamish, a distant relative of Hector. The Laird found out and went for Flora with a knife. She fled to the servants' quarters where Hamish was waiting and the poor old Laird got hit over the head and his throat cut. The other servants covered for Flora and Hamish and they continued to live happily together until Hamish's death and then Flora's some twenty years later.

I find it slightly unfair that they have come back as their younger selves, while I seem to be stuck in my late fifties wearing a nightie and a dressing gown, but I suppose I shouldn't complain. I don't feel the cold any more. I did ask them whether the Laird was around, but apparently if you die a violent death you don't get to haunt. So much for Hector's theory and all those images of headless corpses wandering around with their heads under their arms.

I didn't mean to scare Brian and Celia, but in the early days I hadn't quite got the hang of this walking through walls thing. Apparently you can only go where there has previously been a door or an opening of some kind, not just willy-nilly. Anyway, there were a few bumps and bangs. I think my knocking over the tallboy was the final straw and they've decided to sell up. They're moving out next week and heading back to London. I'm quite disappointed in them. I don't think a few strange noises in the night would have scared me away. What kind of a fool believes in ghosts?

THE VIEWERS

❧

Margaret Quinn

I WATCH THE ESTATE AGENT OPEN the front door to the latest viewers: a family of four wait on the step. Well, at the moment they are four; mister and missus and two children, a boy and girl, but although *she* doesn't realise it yet, I know that missus is expecting again. They look excited and eager; cheeks pink, breath hanging in the autumn air, eyes bright with anticipation; unlike many potential buyers who believe that looking keen might increase the asking price, so try to appear unimpressionable and bored. I like this family on sight, but it's the agent who'll do the business and they don't notice me.

After introductions, we begin the tour. Mr and Mrs Gordon appear pleasantly impressed with the house – a gracious Victorian semi-detached villa with most of its original features: deep skirtings and moulded dados, picture rails and decorative plaster cornices. They enthuse about all the features I've cherished for years, but are tactfully critical about the wall-to-wall dressed stone in the parlour – I mean lounge – displaying a gas miser, ugh! instead of the lovely carved mahogany mantelpiece and surround with its prettily tiled hearth – all wantonly ripped out in the philistine fifties.

Their preferences endear them to me immediately. I've looked after this house for so long. I always live in hopes – if you'll pardon the expression – that new owners would, like me, love it as it was – or rather used to be – and treat it with the respect it deserves, but there's no accounting for taste, and I would have no control over anything they might plan, should they decide they want it.

I shudder as I recall last week's viewer who planned to strip it of the moulded covings and doors and put in laminate floors ... you know, the stuff we see on TV all the time now in this present climate of minimalism. Ikea has never had it so good! I can understand that in a hutch-sized semi with egg-carton rooms, lack of clutter and spacesaving fittings would be essential, but this house was built when space wasn't at a premium, with high, airy rooms and craftsmanship every-where. If you want minimalism, why choose a gracious period place with charm and then strip it all away?

However, I have a gift – rather, a secret weapon – for when unwelcome viewers start to look around: I concentrate hard and *emanate* like mad. I'm good at it actually; I give out as much coldness, damp smells and feelings of inhospitality as I can. I often manage to encourage black beetles to appear. You name it and I'll do it, so long as it's intangible. Once, when an unsympathetic couple were viewing, planning dire modernisation, I managed a cluster of cockroaches! A shout and they were gone – viewers and agent together! How the right or wrong atmosphere can affect judgement. Sorry, but I'm too old-fashioned to put up with that kind of interference.

The Gordons' lively children can't wait to get into the garden. I like that they asked permission before peeling away, showing control and good manners. I've seen hordes of undisciplined youngsters rampaging about, crashing pedal cars and tricycles into doors and skirting, kicking newel posts, running Matchbox cars down the oak banister without being checked. Chipped paint is one thing, but cracked door panels and broken panes of old stained glass, put in when the house was built, are something else – irreplaceable! One viewer on seeing the brass handles and etched panels from the lobby door muttered, 'Bring a mint on eBay.' What a nerd! (I got that word from the TV.) I emanated very hard against him. It worked.

Mister and missus have followed the children outside. The laburnum has shed most of its leaves, and I'm worried that they might say it would have to come out in case the children ate the poisonous pods. I have to say, there was someone who was poisoned in that precise way, by seeds from that very tree, but I'm probably the only one who knows. I see from newspapers and TV that forensic science has only come into its heyday in the last twenty or thirty years. I do love those forensic detectives you see on TV. Nobody would get away with laburnum poisoning nowadays, would they?

I'm pleased to hear the Gordons exclaim on how lovely it must look in the spring, with its blossom-drenched branches. Obviously they know the tree's poisonous nature, but have trained the children never to eat anything from a bush, tree or plant without checking first. The girl Marian, a nice old-fashioned name (after her grandmother), is eight. I can see James, only six, is a little live wire, and warmed to him when I saw him eyeing the wild pear tree. I do like little lads – much more fun than girls with their dollies and make-up. Luckily, that tree is big, old, thick-trunked and impervious to the scrambling and swinging of little tearaways. There hasn't ever been a serious accident during the long years I've resided here. He'll have lots of fun in spite of the scrapes and bruises and they'll all love it when its boughs explode with white spring blossom.

They are all thrilled at the large garden and talk about swings and a paddling pool, but they'll change their minds when she knows about the baby. Mister sees the garden hut as ideal for bicycles and tools. The place looks rather drab on this bleak day and needs imagination to give it life and interest, but even so, the parents can see its potential and they adore the laburnum and pear. I know they'll put in an offer, and the figure they have in mind won't disappoint the agents – just so long as no one comes up with better!

When their offer eventually came I was so relieved. I knew they wanted this place, but it depended on what they could afford after all. Present house prices would have been unimaginable in my day, but that was another life ago. I really don't know how couples manage when starting out now. I learned from subsequent agents' visits, that it would probably be accepted quickly as there was no 'chain'. I've learned all about house buying from TV, you see. I knew if their offer was successful, they hoped to be in before Christmas. I wondered if they could sense my delight.

The shock came a week later. The agent brought a lately-come viewer; a professional type. I had a bad feeling. He didn't see the artisanship: the design of exquisite ceiling covings, spacious landings and elegant French windows opening to the garden, or the wide bay windows. He was interested only in the possibility of removing and adding walls to turn it into – horror of horrors – a dental surgery! All he wanted was the space and solidity of the place, accommodating the provision of as many rooms as he and his partners needed: ceilings dropped to conserve heat; kitchen divided to provide a watercloset – oh, all right, nowadays it's a loo. The elegant parlour, or lounge, as it's called now, was to be a reception and waiting room. Spacious bedrooms were to become separate surgeries which needed plumbing installed for sinks for bleeding, groaning patients to spit into. I'd seen it all on TV in *My Family* where Robert Lindsay was a dentist. But this! I could hardly bear his thoughts. Even worse, the offer was going to be good. Something had to be done quickly!

I emanated like a demon possessed. I breathed bad smells into every room, released the odour of escaping gas, made drains smell, got mice to leave droppings everywhere, called in the beetles; I even induced quite a few of the cockroaches to appear on cue when he re-inspected. The dastardly dentist wasn't unduly put out, alas.

Then, oh joy! A flash of realisation – I remembered the Woodfords next door. Mister W. worked in town planning. If the only weapon I had was to emanate, then I would do it as I'd never ever done before.

That night, I slid through the upstairs dividing wall into the Woodfords' bedroom. I'd never done that before, but needs must when the devil drives, I told myself, so I emanated into Mr W.'s dreams. Poor man, I turned them to nightmares. In his sleep he heard the drills, smelled the blood, foresaw the mess and noise of reconstruction around him. The most effective was the one showing how patients caused parking problems. I'd never experienced this myself, but seemingly they were a major issue in planning departments. Poor Woodford's dreams showed him no space to park his car. Ever.

Although he had not known about the most recent interest in the house next door, Woodford, by a wonderful coincidence, played golf with the estate agent. So real were his dreams that he found himself relating them to his golf partner the following Sunday.

'They'll never get planning of course. Never in a thousand years. I'd see to it personally.' And he smashed the ball viciously. I saw his dream and applauded.

The agent never even mentioned the dental partners' interest to him.

Eventually the dreaded offer was made but overlooked in favour of the Gordons' as I saw that night. I left Mr Woodford to regain his former sleeping patterns and, soon, my favoured family came back and began to take measurements. I relaxed and waited.

They moved in shortly before Christmas, as hoped. I am overjoyed. The dear old place will resound with children's voices again. I've missed that for such a long time. There have been no youngsters around for years and the house has been too quiet for too long.

I realise with pleasure that there will be children's programmes on TV – noisy, bouncy, garish, funny. I can't wait! During the late owner's occupation, there had only ever been snatches, glimpsed briefly as she switched channels. I feel excited as I look forward to all the new programmes I'll be watching with them. The best is yet to come.

→⋙ ⋘←

It's almost Christmas! I watched the tree brought in, decorated and then to my amazement, lit up as I'd never seen before – except in TV films – they call them movies now, of course. Strings of lights twinkling and flickering away like a sky full of multicoloured stars! At first, I stayed up all night just watching and only drifted off when the newly installed timer switched them off after everyone was asleep.

Tonight is Christmas Eve. We're all in the parlour – sorry, lounge. Missus knows she's expecting and says she doesn't want to know what it is, but I'm glad it's to be a boy – another little scallywag, just like James.

I watch the children hang their stockings above the fireplace. Not over that ugly 1950s gas miser with its tombstone overhang, but a real, specially sought-for mahogany surround with an attractive cast-iron insert and some delightful art-nouveau hearth tiles. There are amazing-looking burning logs in the fireplace, too. Gas, would you believe? I've cleaned many a ploppy, smelly gas fire in my time, but I've never seen one looking so real before. The twentieth century certainly produced some wonderful inventions!

Now, I'm comfortably seated between the children – how I wish they could feel my arms around them – and we're watching the animated version of *A Christmas Carol*. I feel so content as I look around the room. Their parents have worked really hard at redressing some of the mistakes made over the years. Mind you, I did have doubts about them removing the dado rail, but the lounge does look nice now, especially with that fire – and the new 42-inch LCD television. Magic!

THE BRIDGE TOLL

Paul Taylor

IT'S KNOWN LOCALLY AS THE SUICIDE BRIDGE, and not without reason. Since opening to carriages and foot traffic just over a century ago, more than four hundred poor souls have clambered over its railings and flung themselves into the turbid waters, some two hundred and fifty feet below. Miraculously, a few survived the fall: but only a few. The majority died from broken necks or by drowning or, most gruesomely of all, suffocating in the banks of grey-brown silt that emerge from the river twice daily at low tide.

At least, that's what the guy in the pub told me. Of course, there was every chance he'd sussed out that I was a visitor to the city and was just spinning a yarn to get a pint out of me. In which case, it had worked.

I handed him his refilled glass and sat down opposite him

at the small, round table. 'So, how come you know so much about the bridge?'

He took a long slurp from the glass then lowered it on to a damp-looking beermat. 'I work on it, son. Been a toll taker for near on twenty-five years. Since I came back from the war.'

'I was at Arnhem,' he added. 'Royal Army Service Corps.'

'Another bridge,' I said. 'They've obviously played a big part in your life.' He looked surprised, as if the thought had never occurred to him.

'You a hippy?' he asked. 'One of them flower people?'

I shrugged. 'Something like that.'

'Thought you were.' He looked pointedly at my hair. 'Into all that free love stuff, are you?'

I shook my head. 'Not really. At least, not since I met Charlie.'

He eyed me suspiciously.

'Short for Charlotte,' I reassured him.

He raised the glass to his lips and took another slurp. 'So where's she to, this Charlie of yours?'

'Back in London. She's helping organise a rally ... against the war in Vietnam.'

'So how come you're here and not there with her?'

Good question.

'My old man offered me fifty quid to come down here for a few days to do a job for him,' I explained. 'And we need the money.'

He let out a whistle. 'Fifty quid? Bloody Nora, that's near on a fortnight's wages. What's he want you to do, rob a bank?'

I laughed. 'His old business partner died recently and left him his house in his will. He wants me to make an inventory of the contents.'

'Live round these parts, did he, this …?'

'Redvers Mandeville,' I said. 'Yeah. Just around the corner … on Sion Hill.'

The toll taker was obviously impressed. 'Nice. Very nice,' he said. 'Place like that'll fetch a pretty penny if your dad decides to sell. This Mandeville bloke must have thought a lot of him.'

I drained my half pint of 'Natch' and set down the empty glass.

'Actually,' I said, 'he hated his guts. They hadn't spoken since before I was born. Mandeville claimed that my father stole my mother from him. I think they were engaged or something and she broke it off to marry my old man.'

'So why'd he leave him his house?'

I shrugged. 'No idea. To mend fences? Heal old wounds?'

He nodded slowly. 'Mebbe. Folk do that when they know they're dying.'

'Yeah, but that's what's so weird,' I said. 'He *didn't* know. My father got to see a transcript of the inquest. The coroner said there was no sign of illness or injury, no drugs or poison in his system. He was a perfectly healthy fifty-five year old.'

The man stiffened and shifted uncomfortably. 'So … what *did* he die of?'

I shrugged. 'No one knows. His housekeeper found him when she went in to clean. He must have died some time the evening before because he was sitting in his armchair, rigid, his eyes wide open, as if he'd seen a —'

The toll taker pushed back his chair and stood up abruptly. His face was ashen. 'I'd best be getting back to work.'

'But you haven't finished your drink,' I said, pointing to his half-full glass.

But he either didn't hear me, or chose not to, because without another word he pushed his way through the busy bar and disappeared into the street, leaving the pub door to slam shut behind him.

'Not like Den to leave good beer undrunk. Whatever d'you say to him?'

I turned. It was the landlord; he was collecting empties from the table behind me.

'No idea,' I replied truthfully. 'He just kind of … freaked out.'

I spent the rest of the afternoon wandering around Clifton Village, enjoying the autumn sunshine. I used five bob of the money my father had given me to buy some basic provisions from a small corner shop: a jar of coffee, a bottle of milk, a loaf of bread, a couple of apples and some cheese. I only intended staying for two days at the most, so I just needed a few essentials to keep body and soul together. And, anyway, there was always the pub round the corner if I fancied a pie or another half of their brain-rotting cider.

At around five, I returned to the house on Sion Hill and let myself in with the key my father had given me. The narrow frontage was deceptive; beyond the porticoed entrance was an impressive home laid out over four floors with a wine cellar and scullery in the basement, a reception room and kitchen on the ground floor, a spacious sitting room and study on the first, and three bedrooms and a bathroom at the top of the house. Every room had been lavishly furnished and decorated with works of art: mostly nineteenth-century landscapes and paintings of horses. It wasn't exactly my kind of thing – in those days, I was more into the whole Pop Art scene – but even I could tell that the collection must be worth a small fortune.

I headed for the kitchen, boiled a kettle of water and made myself a mug of coffee then climbed the stairs to the first floor. I had no real plan in mind for cataloguing the contents of the house, but Mandeville's study seemed as good a starting point as any.

I took a notepad and pen from my canvas shoulder bag, slung the bag on to a nearby chair, and turned my attention to the big mahogany desk that dominated the book-lined room.

There was nothing on it, apart from a brass desk calendar and a few art gallery catalogues, so I decided to try the drawers. The first two contained nothing more than a pair of reading glasses in a case, a train timetable, a copy of *Wisden*, a few bulldog clips and some headed stationery. The third – the bottom drawer – was empty except for a hand-addressed envelope.

I picked it up. In the top left-hand corner, underlined twice, was the word PRIVATE. Scrawled across the middle of the envelope were the words:

For the personal attention of Robert Fuller Esq.

Robert Fuller. My father.

I took my mug of coffee and, still staring at the envelope, wandered into the adjoining room. I decided against sitting in the chair where Mandeville had died – more out of superstition than respect – and instead opened the French windows and stepped out onto the wrought iron balcony that overhung the front door and the steps leading down to the basement. A high-backed rattan chair had been positioned to take full advantage of the view, and I settled myself in it, causing the woven cane to creak ominously.

I set my mug down on the small glass-topped table beside the chair and gazed at the bridge: the tops of its stone towers were glowing in the light of the setting sun like two enormous beacons. I leaned forward and put my eye to the eyepiece of the brass telescope that was mounted onto the balcony's railings. Mandeville had obviously spent a lot of time out here, in his eyrie, observing the bridge. I swung the telescope, following a pair of crows as they wheeled in and out of the bridge's cables. I watched them until they disappeared under the great sweep of its deck, heading for the wooded slopes on the far side of the gorge.

I sat back in the chair and looked again at the envelope. It struck me that the contents might be personal, and I wondered if I should call my father to ask him if he wanted me to send the letter on to him. But the telephone in the house had been cut off – I knew; I'd tried to call Charlie earlier – and the nearest phone box I'd seen was on the far side of the green, a good ten-minute walk away.

'Sorry, Pops.'

I slid my thumb under the flap and tore open the envelope. The letter was written on the same headed notepaper I'd seen in the top drawer of the desk. The handwriting was shaky, almost illegible, and it took me a good five minutes to decipher the unsteady scrawl.

Robert,
I write this letter to you in the certain knowledge that I will soon be dead.

As you are undoubtedly already aware, I have recently amended my will with the intention of leaving you my house and all of its contents. You may, of course, dispose of them as you wish, but I would be gratified to think that you might spend at least a few days here, in what was my home of twenty years, enjoying the congenial surroundings and the splendid view of Brunel's great structure.

(Regarding the bridge: I would urge you strongly to observe it through my old Negretti and Zambra telescope, at dusk, when the moon is full; only then can certain eccentricities of the structure be seen to their best advantage.)

Please pass on my best wishes to Rachel and tell her that I wish her every happiness for the future.

Your one-time friend,

Redvers

I re-folded the letter, tucked it back into the envelope and placed it on the table next to my mug of now-cold coffee.

So, Mandeville *had* known that he was going to die. But with illness and suicide ruled out as the cause of death, how was that possible? And why had he been so insistent that my father should come here, to this house, to view the bridge?

Observe it through my old Negretti and Zambra telescope, at dusk, when the moon is full.

I looked up. The moon was high, but only half full. Even so, its pale light was enough to make the bridge appear luminous against the darkening sky.

I put my eye to the telescope again and slowly scanned the length of the bridge. A car crossed, followed by another. Then stillness. I waited, hardly breathing, hoping to spot the *eccentricities of the structure* that Mandeville had mentioned.

I was just about to give up and return to the warmth of the sitting room when a figure walked into my field of view. I turned the knurled focusing ring. It was a young woman, about my age, dressed in a canary yellow coat. I watched her pass the tollbooths on the Clifton side and head on to the bridge. The image juddered slightly as I followed her progress and I realised that my hand was trembling.

It was as she neared the midpoint that I saw, or thought I saw, something move ... something on the *underside* of the bridge's deck. I told myself that it was nothing more than a shadow or a smudge on the lens – how could it be anything else? But then the shadow edged into the moonlight, and I knew without doubt that the thing – whatever it was – was real.

With a mounting sense of dread, I watched it pause, as if waiting for the girl to pass overhead.

Then, with uncanny speed and agility, it crawled over the railings on to the walkway behind her.

I leapt out of the chair and screamed at the top of my voice, 'RUN! GET THE HELL OUT OF THERE – RUN!'

The girl must have heard me, because she turned. But it was too late: the thing was already on her. For a moment she disappeared into the shadows, then I caught a glimpse of her yellow coat as her attacker lifted her effortlessly into the air and flung her over the bridge railings.

I watched her fall, arms and legs flailing, until she disappeared from sight.

'Dear God, NO!' I cried out.

And that was when the thing turned to look in my direction.

Without thinking, I fled through the house. I vaulted down the stairs and, throwing open the front door, sprinted across the road and over the manicured grass, heading for the bridge and the toll taker's booth.

I hammered on the booth's window, startling the uniformed man behind the glass.

'A girl,' I shouted at him breathlessly. 'Someone … some*thing* just threw a girl off the bridge.'

He looked at me as if I was crazy, but, grabbing a flashlight, opened the door and hurried behind me as I half-stumbled, half-ran along the walkway. We reached the middle of the bridge and stopped in our tracks; lying on the floor were a shoulder bag and a single white shoe. We both leaned over the railings and stared down into the darkness. Far below, I could just make out a small, yellow shape bobbing in the moonlit water.

'Bloody hell,' said the toll taker. 'I just saw her walk past my booth. Pretty little thing, she was. What makes someone like that want to do herself in?'

I stared at him, incredulous. 'She didn't *do herself in*!' I exclaimed. 'I told you ... something came from underneath the bridge. It grabbed hold of her and threw her over the side. I saw it happen.'

But it was as if he couldn't hear me.

'My first jumper,' he said with a sigh. 'S'pose I'd better close the bridge and call the police.'

We left the bag and shoe where they were and walked back to his booth in silence. He made the call, then took my name and address in case the police wanted to question me, although he seemed to think it unlikely.

'They don't bother interviewing witnesses,' he told me. 'Not for jumpers.'

I made my way back to Sion Hill, the image of the falling girl replaying over and over in my head.

I let myself into the house, closed the door behind me and bolted it. Wearily, I climbed the stairs to the first floor and pushed open the door to the sitting room. As I did, a wave of nausea swept over me: the air was thick with the foetid stink of stagnant water. I gripped the doorframe to steady myself, but, as I did, something caught my eye, and my heart began to pound. There were footprints on the carpet – bare footprints, with grey mud trailing behind them.

'Oh dear God.'

It had been there ... in that room ... the thing from the bridge. And in that instant I knew that this wasn't the first time. Mandeville had seen it, too: had been a witness to it killing.

And because of that it had come for him.

That was why he'd left the house to my father: not to make amends, but to take revenge on him, in the hope that he would suffer the same dreadful fate.

A sudden creak made me look up. There was someone on the balcony. The rattan creaked again as a figure rose slowly from the chair. I started to shake uncontrollably. The French windows began to swing open, and a hand reached into the room: a long, fleshless hand, slathered with mud. I let out a strangled cry and, in a blind panic, turned and ran.

I ran from that house and never looked back.

⋙ ⋘

That night has haunted me for forty-five years.

No one believed my story. No one, that is, apart from my lovely Charlotte. And now that she is gone, now that I have nothing left to live for, I have returned to the bridge one last time.

It is dusk. The moon is full.

The bridge itself has hardly changed. The toll takers have been replaced by automated coin collectors, and there are barriers now along the bridge's length; high wire ones to prevent those without hope from ending their lives with a final flight into oblivion. But barriers won't stop *it*. Nothing will.

I make my way to the middle of the bridge, to the point where the colossal support chains sweep down to almost touch the deck, and I prepare.

Ten minutes pass, maybe fifteen. I look back down towards the lights of the houses on Sion Hill, and wonder if anyone is watching me. I hope not, for their sake.

And then it comes. The hand from my nightmares appears out of the darkness and clutches the railing. The smell of decay fills my nostrils. Trembling, I press the button. A figure rises up in front of me: a hate-filled thing of mud and shadow. I catch a fleeting glimpse of a gaunt, hollow-eyed face, its teeth bared in a mirthless grin. Then the thing reaches out. It takes hold of me, lifts me into the air and flings me, screaming, over the barrier and into the void.

I see the dark ribbon of the river rushing towards me and I close my eyes. I pray that the video camera taped to the support chain is still recording.

This time they *will* believe me.

THE GHOSTS OF SKINNER'S HALL

Anne Ayres

KATE AWOKE TO DAZZLING SUNSHINE. She lay perfectly still, letting her eyes roam around the unfamiliar room. Yesterday there had been the confusion of moving house. Today was the start of their new life. Kate smiled and rolled over in bed to share the thought with Matt. He was already awake, head propped up on one arm looking at her.

'Good morning, sleepyhead,' he said, leaning forward to kiss her.

'What time is it?' she asked, looking for the alarm clock on a bedside table that wasn't there.

'Haven't you noticed something?' Matt raised a quizzical eyebrow.

'Apart from the chaos, you mean?'

'Listen.' Matt put a finger to his lips and shushed.

'I can't hear anything.'

'Exactly.'

Wonderment spread across Kate's face, to be replaced by a look of horror. She struggled into a sitting position.

'My God, is he all right? I knew we shouldn't have put him into a room by himself in a strange house. He's just a baby.'

She scrabbled to get out of bed, her heart thumping in panic.

'Calm down, it's fine. I've been to check. Charlie's sleeping like a lamb. The house seems to have cured him of his early morning miseries.'

Kate sank back in relief, and then a new thought overtook her.

'Do you have to go into work today? You ought to have a day off for moving house.'

She looked at him hopefully, but she already knew the answer. Without his demanding job, with its long hours, they couldn't have afforded the mortgage on Cragside.

They had both fallen in love with the house right away. It was a rambling grey stone building seeming to sprout organically from a granite outcrop. The architecture embraced the many styles favoured by its previous owners. The end result was original and charming. It stood a little apart from the village, with breathtaking views over the undulating moors and the lake lying in the valley below. They had first visited it, estate agent's leaflet in hand, on a perfect spring day when

marshmallow clouds raced across a clear blue sky. An inter-
mittent sun shone over the green haze of new growth, and
Kate had wanted to stretch out and embrace it. From the
other side of the house the view was more mundane. Beyond
the village they could see the distant roofscape of the town
where Matt's company had its offices. A half-hour drive would
see him safely at work.

After Matt left, Kate felt overwhelmed by the boxes piled
up in every room. She got Charlie up, dressed and breakfasted
and decided to escape.

'Let's go for a walk, Charlie,' she said. 'Let's go exploring.'

Charlie, rusk in hand, gave a gummy grin of assent. She
popped him into his pushchair, locked the front door and
set off. She tried to ignore the garden, which was even more
chaotic than the house. Roses and brambles crawled over each
other and nettles sprouted in between what might have been
proper plants.

It didn't take her long to walk through the village. It had
one main street with several side turnings that led nowhere
and petered out. There was a pub, a grocer's, a church with
services held on the third Sunday of each month and a village
hall with a toddlers' group on Tuesdays and a youth club on
Fridays. She saw there were other notices pinned to a board,
but they were faded and curled with age.

Outside the grocer's she met Gladys Walters, an angular
woman with a nose for gossip. Kate could almost sense her

quivering with excitement when she realised she was the first to meet the village's new resident.

'So, how are you finding Cragside?' she asked, after initial introductions had been made. 'It's not everyone's cup of tea. It's out on a limb and you'll have heard about the things that have happened there.'

'We love it,' Kate said, deliberately not taking the bait.

'I hope you'll be very happy, I'm sure. The last two families didn't stay long.'

'We don't plan moving anywhere,' Kate said firmly. 'We want Charlie to grow up here.'

Mrs Walters looked doubtfully down at Charlie in his pushchair.

'If you need anything, you'll find me at Church Lane, number five. The cottage with the blue door,' she added, as though there might have been doubt about the numbering system.

Kate returned home and carried Charlie up the stairs.

'Time for a morning nap, my boy,' she said.

She opened the door to his room to find the curtains flapping wildly and a blast of ice cold air enveloping her. She gasped and Charlie screamed at the shock of it. She lay him down quickly in his cot despite his cries of outrage and went to shut the window.

'I don't think I left that open,' she said, half to Charlie and half to reassure herself. 'No, I'm sure I didn't.'

She straightened the curtains, faded blue cotton ones left by the previous owners, and then went over to Charlie's cot. He lay on his back, staring intently at something over Kate's left shoulder. He was smiling and turning his head away coyly before wriggling excitedly. Kate turned, half expecting to see Matt, but there was nothing there.

'What can you see, Charlie?' she asked, but as he turned to look at her the smile melted from his lips.

'Let's tuck you in. That wind was cold, wasn't it?'

Her talk was inconsequential and gradually his eyes grew heavy and he slept.

When Matt got home, she told him about the window being open, but now it sounded trivial. Her husband was tired after a long day at the computer face, and the mystery of whether a sash window could rise by itself failed to interest him.

And so the first week passed. Gradually boxes were unpacked and possessions were arranged around the house. A couple of new neighbours came to introduce themselves and offer help if any were needed. They declined invitations to come inside for a cup of tea. Kate put it down to their good manners, the house still being in less than pristine order.

Over the weekend, the weather turned warm. Monday morning was oppressive, with lowering skies that threatened a storm. Charlie was restlessly asleep upstairs. Kate was leaning on the kitchen sink watching an unfolding drama taking place outside the window as towering black clouds rolled in over the moors. She could see her own reflection in the glass, and then she saw a figure sweep past the doorway behind her and disappear along the hallway. She spun around and caught a glimpse of grey and a flutter of something white. She shrieked, her hand flying to her mouth to suppress the sound. The shock rendered her immobile, but she forced herself to move to protect Charlie.

'Who's there?' she called, her voice trembling nervously, and then: 'How dare you come into my house?'

Anger made her sound stronger. She ran up the stairs, two at a time, and into Charlie's room. The window stood wide open to the elements. The curtains fluttered wildly and eddies of sultry air swirled around the nursery. She frantically started opening cupboards and knelt to look under furniture, but there was no one there. Charlie lay smiling adoringly at something that Kate couldn't see. She swept him up in her arms and hugged him so hard that he yelled in protest. Her legs suddenly gave way and she sat down heavily on the junior bed that Charlie had yet to grow into. Outside the storm broke. Thunder rolled ominously overhead and lightning flashed at the open window. She and Charlie huddled together taking comfort from each other. She thought she ought to phone Matt, but the moment passed. He would just think she had lost it, couldn't cope on her own.

The following day, at the grocer's, she got into conversation with Mrs Absalom, a frail old lady with bright, intelligent eyes.

'Are you settling into Cragside?' she asked. 'Getting on all right, are you?' She tilted her head on one side like an inquisitive robin.

'We love it,' Kate said loyally, and then the words slipped from her mouth. 'But things keep happening. Little things, stupid things.'

'Ah,' Mrs Absalom nodded. 'I expect they do. I'm afraid Cragside has something of a reputation. My grandfather was gardener to Major Skinner and his wife. It was called "Skinner's Hall" then, named for a family who worked sheep hides in the dim and distant past. The Major enjoyed the conceit of the name, sounded like his ancestral home. After the trouble they thought a change of name would make people forget, but it didn't.'

'Forget what?'

Mrs Absalom shrugged. 'Never been a happy place. There's always been talk.'

'About what?'

The old lady shook her head regretfully and moved away before turning back again. 'You should ask the vicar. Ask him about the children.'

Mrs Absalom gave her a strange look, and even though the sun was shining, a chill ran through Kate's body. That night she told Matt about it, but he wasn't impressed. He dismissed it as 'the ramblings of a batty old woman'.

It was exactly a week later when Kate heard faint singing coming from Charlie's room. She burst into the nursery and the thread of song evaporated. The window was open again, but the curtains only fluttered gently in the summer breeze. Charlie was standing in his cot, a puzzled expression on his face, his eyes roaming the room looking for something or someone.

'Here I am,' Kate said, stretching out her arms to him, but his face crumpled in disappointment, his mouth turning down at the corners. Outside she heard children's laughter.

'Let's see who's there,' she said to the baby to distract him. They peered through the window, but there was no one there. She took Charlie downstairs and put the radio on to dispel her unease. She didn't let him out of her sight for the rest of the day.

That night she told Matt that Charlie was going to sleep in their room.

'He's happy in his own room,' Matt said wearily. Kate wouldn't be dissuaded. 'I want him to be with us,' she said firmly.

But Charlie was determined to have his say. He worked himself up into a hysterical tantrum, his face turning puce and his little body racked with sobs. In the end, frightened that he would harm himself, Matt moved the cot back into the nursery. Right away Charlie was wreathed in smiles and settled down to sleep.

On her next walk around the village, Kate came across the vicar labouring in the churchyard. He was attacking a tangle of growth around the gravestones with an inadequate pair of shears.

'You can't get anyone to do this sort of work.'

He had grinned up at her. Kate was surprised. She had assumed that in a village there would be no shortage of volunteers.

'There are no relatives left to look after the old graves so I'm afraid it's up to me. Families die out,' he said, voicing the inevitable.

'I met Mrs Absalom the other day,' said Kate. 'She said I should ask you about our house, Cragside, or I think she said it used to be called Skinner's Hall.'

'Ah yes.' The vicar took out a hanky and mopped his glistening brow. He put down the shears and leaned against a convenient headstone.

'You mustn't take too much notice of the local folklore. It's a throwback to an age before television. Nothing like a few ghoulish stories to entertain a gathering on a dark winter's evening.' He laughed. 'Only wish they'd pay the same attention to my sermons.'

He fumbled in his pockets and took out a pipe.

'You don't mind if I light up, do you? I know it's not PC, but I'm old-fashioned.'

Kate and the vicar stood in companionable silence. Across

the moorland a curlew called out, a hauntingly lonely sound. Nearby small creatures scuttled in the undergrowth and the wind rustled the long grass. Charlie watched a fluttering butterfly and conducted an invisible orchestra with his strong little arms.

'What a dear chap,' the vicar said, pointing at him with his pipe.

'Mrs Absalom said to ask you about the children.'

'Sad affair, that. All a bit lost in the mists of time now, but according to the locals it was all to do with the nursery maid. When she took the children out for their walks she met up with her young man. Got up to no good if the gossips are to be believed. One day, when the maid was otherwise engaged, the children wandered off and drowned in the lake. The poor girl took her own life in remorse.'

The vicar paused, and then looked Kate straight in the eye.

'It's got everything, hasn't it? Crime, punishment, sex and death. The rumour is that Agnes's ghost walks looking for the children. Of course, if they're all dead I would have thought she would have known where they were.'

He gave a short bark of laughter, making Charlie jump.

'And is any of it true?'

The vicar shrugged his shoulders.

'There's certainly a headstone naming two children, John and Lydia Skinner, who died on the same day in 1912. It's not actually clear how they died because the parish records are incomplete. It's very sad, but as for wraiths walking the moors I should put that right out of your head.'

'What about the family? What happened to them?'

'They say the mother went mad with grief and had to be locked away. Although, and again this is local gossip, she had always been a little odd. Two years later and the major was lost at Ypres. It really is the stuff of grand opera.'

The vicar shook his head sadly and tapped out his pipe.

'Have you and Charlie joined the toddlers' group yet?' he continued, moving on to a safer subject. 'Not many youngsters in this village, but a few mums come from the outlying farms. You two would be a welcome addition, I'm sure.'

That night Kate told Matt about Agnes and the children.

'And you think that's what's been going on here?' he asked her incredulously. A life spent in offices with state-of-the-art technology didn't lend itself to a belief in things that go bump in the night.

'I saw a grey dress,' Kate said stubbornly. 'And someone keeps opening the window in the nursery. They believed in plenty of fresh air in the old days.'

'You don't seem frightened any more.'

'No,' Kate said thoughtfully. 'Isn't it strange? Now I know about Agnes I feel she wants to look after Charlie, not hurt him. Does that make sense?'

'Well, if it makes you feel any better ...' Matt let the sentence trail off. 'Come on, let me give you a hug,' he said, suiting his actions to the words. 'I'm not sure that living in the country is agreeing with you.'

'I'm fine,' she said, and at that moment she truly believed it.

The next day was Friday. Kate was looking forward to Matt being home for the weekend. They had plans for decorating and doing something with the garden. Matt had some daft idea about buying a dog for Charlie and wanted to go and visit a farm that had puppies for sale. Kate wasn't so sure. It sounded like more work to her.

She was sitting at the kitchen table, all their plans swimming pleasantly around her head, when she heard the footsteps. They were coming from above in Charlie's room. And the singing had started up again. Now she could make out the words.

'*Rock a bye baby on the tree top.*'

She imagined Agnes pacing the floor, carrying Charlie and rocking him off to sleep. She ran up the stairs almost joyfully.

'Agnes,' she called out from the landing. 'I know it's you. Come out. Let me see you.'

The words came naturally. She was imagining Agnes wearing a long grey dress and wrapped in a nursery maid's apron. The vision was so vivid she could reach out and touch it. She pushed the nursery door open and caught sight of the edge of the grey skirt as it whisked behind the door and disappeared. She checked on Charlie, and he looked at her with a startled expression.

'Come out, Agnes, please. I want to talk to you.'

Kate searched the room, pulling the curtains aside and peering down the narrow gap at the back of the wardrobe. She went out on to the landing, intending to check the other rooms. The push in her back was sudden and vicious. For agonising seconds she teetered at the top of the stairs. She fought valiantly to regain her balance but it was no good; once set in motion, she tumbled awkwardly down the stairs. Her hands scrabbled uselessly at the banisters and her head banged painfully against the wall. She landed with a sickening thud in the hallway, stunned, unable to move, all the breath knocked out of her.

She was confused with concussion, but she couldn't get the thought out of her head that somehow she'd got it all wrong. And if it wasn't Agnes up there, it could only be the other woman, the mother who went mad.

'Mrs Skinner?' she whispered fearfully.

Above her the singing started up again.

'Rock a bye baby on the tree top.'

She heard Charlie gurgling with pleasure, and children's joyful laughter coming from the garden. She wasn't conscious when the screaming started.

PROFESSOR MOON'S
MAGIC SPELLS

Graham Corcoran

HE WAS JUST AN ORDINARY MAN walking down an ordinary street, but as he turned to enter his favourite bookshop that bright September morning he unwittingly triggered an amazing sequence of events. His name was Alan Bailey and he was 57 years old.

His initial perusal of the books had proved disappointing. It was over six weeks since his last visit, but nothing seemed to have changed. The same dusty titles sitting on the same dusty shelves. Business was obviously slack. It was as he turned to leave that his hitherto normal existence was elevated to the truly bizarre.

The shopkeeper had been leafing through a large, leather-bound volume, which he closed just as Alan walked past the counter. It creaked like an ancient, unused door, and Alan couldn't resist a comment.

'That sounds intriguingly old. What is it?'

The bookman smiled. '*Professor Moon's Magic Spells*.' He turned the book around. 'Take a look.'

Alan, fascinated by anything to do with magic, peered forward eagerly. 'Do any of them actually work?'

The bookman's smile returned, but with it came a knowing sneer that Alan found distasteful. He had never liked the man.

'The memory-erasing spell seems to be in order.'

Alan frowned. 'Seems to be? How can you tell?'

The bookman produced a folded piece of paper from beneath his counter. 'A few moments ago I offered to try out the memory-erasing spell on you. I asked you your wife's favourite film, your mother's maiden name and your father's date of birth. I take it you recall none of this?'

Alan shook his head, hardly believing what he was hearing.

The bookman pushed the folded paper across the counter. 'Here are the answers, exactly as you gave them to me.'

Alan picked up the paper and read the neatly printed words. Suddenly his mouth felt very dry, as a frisson of excitement swept over him. He looked around, but there was no one else to share the moment. He looked again at the book lying on the counter. 'How much do you want for it?' He was trying not to let his enthusiasm show.

The bookman shrugged. 'It's marked up at sixty pounds, but you're a good customer. Shall we say forty?'

Alan reached into his pocket. 'Do the rest of the spells work as well as that one?'

The man frowned. 'I'm not really into magic, sir, but I'll tell you an amusing way to find out. Turn to page thirty-six and have a go at the invisibility spell. Try it on your wife tonight. If it doesn't work, you can have your money back tomorrow. How does that sound?' To Alan it sounded fantastic. And to think, five minutes ago he'd been feeling disappointed. He couldn't wait to get the book home.

The television had been switched off following the news. Rachel Bailey was sitting in the lounge reading one of her seemingly endless stream of fashion magazines. She hardly noticed as Alan slipped out into the hall, deliberately leaving the door half open.

He crept upstairs into the bedroom and picked up his latest acquisition. There was nothing printed on the cover, and nothing inside gave any hint as to who Professor Moon might have been. The spells were presented in a very uneven style which added to the book's mysterious charm. There were no publication details, and Alan wondered if it was a one-off, printed by the professor. He pictured an old man, bearded and frail, toiling away to preserve for ever his fabulous secrets. Alan's fingers trembled as he flipped through the yellowed, musty pages, and for a moment he had the awful feeling that someone – or something – very unclean was in the room with him. He looked around, the skin on his arms crawling, but there was nothing there. How could there be? He shook his head dismissively as he flipped through to page 36. The book stressed that absolute faith was required for any spell to be effective, and that failure to follow the instructions implicitly would 'gravely impair the resultant spell'. He read exactly what he had to do to make himself invisible for a ten-minute duration.

He crept down the stairs, his entire body tingling in anticipation as he approached the half-open lounge door. The book had explained that to the person initiating the spell there would be no change in appearance. He would, it seemed, be invisible to all but himself.

If this worked – and it was essential that he believed it would – the world would never be the same again. He paused at the lounge door and took a deep breath before easing himself gently into the room.

Ten minutes later he was back upstairs in the bedroom, his skin wet with perspiration, his heart pounding. What an incredible, mind-blowing investment that book had been.

It worked! The invisibility spell actually worked! He'd

entered the lounge in a state of unbearable suspense, desperate for proof of his success before lack of faith got the better of him. He'd stood in front of Rachel and placed his open palm across her eyes, blocking her view of the magazine. Except that it hadn't blocked the magazine at all. He'd waved his hand up and down, inches from her face, and her eyes hadn't flickered. He'd almost shouted 'Yes!' and punched the air, but just about held himself back. Then he'd bent down and his legs had creaked, and for one horrid moment she'd looked up from her wretched magazine and their eyes had met. He'd held his breath, not daring to move, until at last she'd looked down again, totally oblivious as he waved a clenched fist in her face, his confidence now fully restored. It was all he could do to pull himself away and creep back up the stairs before the spell wore off.

⊷⊶

During the next three days, Alan spent as much time as he could studying the strange book. He still didn't feel at ease with it, but his enthusiasm always overcame his unexplainable reluctance to delve within its incredible pages. There were spells for controlling the temper and increasing one's stamina. Spells for encouraging fertility and easing toothache. There was one for creating fog and another for dispersing it. Many of the spells were more than a little disturbing. One showed how to induce frenzy in a crowded room. Another offered total submission. Much of it was racist. Whoever Professor Moon was, he was certainly no humanitarian. There was even a spell to take care of unfaithful partners. The idea made Alan smile, but it also made him think. He had been married to Rachel for twenty-one years, but the last five or so had been an uphill struggle.

She was still an attractive woman, but somewhere down the line the fiery independence he'd fallen in love with had changed to a barbed vindictiveness that he now merely tolerated. He had no proof that Rachel was interested in anyone else, but on more than one occasion recently she'd made little cryptic comments in the heat of the moment that made him wonder. This book could come in very useful in the future.

⇥⊷ ⊶⊣

One evening, just after supper, Rachel said, 'Don't forget you were going to check those loose tiles on the roof. The weather forecast isn't looking good.'

Alan groaned. He hated anything involving ladders and roofs. He hated heights. Unless … He rummaged again through the professor's book. Yes, there it was. The antigravity spell. Suddenly, incredibly, he was actually looking forward to the task in hand.

⇥⊷ ⊶⊣

He could hardly believe that he was up on the roof and posi-tively enjoying the experience. Even when he looked down he felt no fear. Only exhilaration. Once or twice he almost slipped, but instead of the gut-wrenching fear that would normally have flooded through him there was simply a grin and a what-the-heck shrug. It was a cold October morning, the sky heavy with the threat of more rain, but nothing could spoil his mood, or dampen his enthusiasm. He had located most of the loose and worn tiles, and what's more he would replace them all himself at a fraction of the cost of hiring a professional roofer. How could he not be cheerful?

Earlier, Rachel had come out of the house to go to the post box, and he wondered what she would have said if he'd just floated down to join her. Because he could. Without a doubt. He'd love to have seen the look on her face, but he still wasn't ready to share the secret. Just thinking about it was good enough for now. Eventually, he did lose his footing, yet even as he tumbled from the roof he had every faith in his own invulnerability. It was only when he was about six feet from the ground and showing no signs of slowing down that blind terror overtook all other emotions. His mouth opened wide, but the only sound he made was a sickening thud as his body hit the driveway.

The owner of the bookshop turned as he heard the bell above

the door tinkle, and he found himself gazing into the clear blue eyes of Rachel Bailey. It had been a week since the funeral. Beneath her arm was a large, leather-bound book.

'I think you ought to have this back,' she said in a slow, quiet voice.

The bookman nodded towards the back room, and the woman moved forward, still clutching the heavy book. As the door closed behind them, she placed the book on the desk before turning to face the shop owner. Her eyes sparkled as she threw herself into his arms. 'I never thought it would happen so soon!' she said in a breathless whisper. The bookman chuckled. 'Was he trying one of the spells, or did he simply fall?'

The woman nodded. 'There was a bookmark by the gravity-defying spell. You should have seen the way he was prancing around on the wet roof. I always knew his gullibility would be his downfall.' She pulled away. 'Tell me, do any of the spells in that book actually work?'

The bookman shrugged. 'I've no idea. Why do you ask?'

She glanced at the book and then looked away quickly. 'I don't know. There's just … something about it that makes my skin crawl. I couldn't have stood it in the house a moment longer.' She shuddered, and again he took her in his arms, but at that moment a sudden, uncomfortable warmth swept over them both. They tried to pull apart, their passion fading rapidly as they discovered that they were unable to do so.

The warmth became an unpleasant, searing heat, yet there was nothing they could do to escape it. Somehow their bodies had become fused together as one. They began to panic as they tried to pull their faces apart, violently, painfully, the awful heat almost unbearable. Now it was unbearable, it was more than flesh and blood and bone could stand, and there was no pleasure or satisfaction for the scheming lovers as they melted in each other's arms.

As suddenly as it had arrived, the killing heat had gone, leaving almost everything in the tiny room twisted and blackened by its ferocity. Only the leather-bound book lay cool and undamaged where Rachel Bailey had laid it on the now scorched desk top. Only moments before, she had asked if any of the spells in the book actually worked. Well, the one that dealt with unfaithful partners certainly did! As for the rest, only one person would know for sure.

Deep within the leaves of his treacherous book, like a vindictive, wary spider, Professor Moon waited patiently for his next visitors to arrive.

A WHITE FEATHER

Gillian Jackson

ANDREW CONLAN WOKE WITH A START, wondering for a moment where he was. He stretched out and kicked against other legs; opening his eyes he saw a clergyman with a frosty expression sitting opposite him.

'I'm sorry, I must have dropped off.'

The woman sitting next to him laughed. 'You certainly did, you were snoring louder than this train.'

Andrew flushed and concentrated on looking out of the window. The red earth of Devon had given way to grey Cornish granite; surely the long journey from London must soon be over. He caught glimpses of the sea sparkling in the September sunshine and the anticipation of beaches and swimming cheered him up. Not that he would have a lot of free time, he reminded himself, teaching in a boys' preparatory school.

He wondered, not for the first time, whether he'd made a mistake accepting the job. He'd been straight with the headmaster during the interview, telling him that he'd left Oxford in the summer of 1939 with a decent degree in history, but that at the outbreak of war he'd been a conscientious objector, spending some months in prison before undertaking essential war work. He'd been sent on deployment to a factory that made parachutes. His life in prison had been wretched, bullied by both prisoners and warders alike. It hadn't been easy in the factory either: many of the women refused to work with a conchie while others had done their best to make his life a misery.

Applicants for teaching posts were still thin on the ground in 1946. Andrew guessed this was why he'd been successful. Christopher Marsden, the headmaster, had finished the interview, in the small London hotel, by shaking his hand and offering him the post of history teacher at St Anthony's Preparatory School for Boys.

His parents had been relieved that he'd found what they called 'a proper job' that would take him far away from them. They wanted nothing more to do with him. They'd been embarrassed and humiliated by his refusal to enter one of the forces, especially his father, who'd fought in the First World War. When neighbours and friends talked of their sons or daughters defending their country, his own parents kept quiet.

He stared through the grimy windows at the passing fields,

forcing himself to concentrate on his new life. The train clacking over the rails rhythmically tapped out the message, goodbye to the past, goodbye to the past, goodbye to the past.

It was dusk when Andrew stepped onto the station platform. He stood shivering while his trunk was unloaded from the guard's van and the train sent on its way with a shrill whistle.

He was relieved to see Marsden's stocky figure coming down the platform towards him.

'Welcome to St Anthony's,' he boomed in his bluff way. 'Let me give you a hand with the luggage.'

Soon, helped by the porter, they were loaded up and trotting through the narrow, winding lanes towards the school.

'It's good of you to meet me, sir.'

Marsden grinned. 'I enjoy driving the trap, it reminds me of my boyhood, and Blackie likes a run around, too.' He clicked his tongue at the horse and it seemed to Andrew that they bowled along at a smarter trot. He held on nervously, not used to horses or this mode of transport.

The school turned out to be a large, dilapidated Georgian mansion set very near to the coast. The grounds ran to the headland from where the sea could be heard battering the rocky beach below.

That evening, after supper, Andrew found himself a corner in the staffroom where he sat nursing a weak cup of coffee. There was a cheerful hubbub of chatter, greetings and reminiscences that ebbed and flowed in the firelight. The cosiness of it all made Andrew feel an outsider.

Through the window he could see the moon, a white circle hung against the deep blue of the night: its indifference comforted him. There was no judgement in its beauty.

He became aware of someone trying to get his attention.

'Sorry; I was daydreaming.'

'We were wondering if you played bridge?' The speaker, a tall, grey-haired man, looked hopeful.

'I'm afraid not.'

'Shame, we were looking for a fourth.' He held out a hand, 'I'm Chivers by the way. I teach the little blighters mathematics.'

Andrew was conscious of the chatter becoming muted. It seemed to him that he was under scrutiny from the whole room. He muttered an excuse about being tired and having to finish unpacking, stumbled to his feet and red with embarrassment made his way out of the room.

There was a moment's silence, and then a voice rang out. 'Extraordinary fellow! What was Marsden thinking of?'

'Probably the best of a bad bunch.'

'Fellow needs a haircut.' This from Bradshaw, the sports master, who'd already put the newcomer down as an effete slacker.

'Pity about the bridge, though,' said Chivers.

As he climbed the stairs up to his room, Andrew cursed himself for being a fool. Why couldn't he have offered to learn bridge, make a joke of it, anything rather than rushing off like an idiot.

As he turned on to the landing the lights flickered and went out. He couldn't see anything. The darkness seemed impenetrable. He stood, heart thumping, straining to see.

Gradually his eyes adjusted and a faint ray of moonlight revealed dark doorways lining the passage. It was then he thought he would pass out with terror. He saw eyes watching him. A myriad of them, stretching down the corridor. They didn't blink or move, just watched him, as though marking him, assessing him.

The moonlight brightened as a cloud passed revealing portraits lining the walls. The figures were shadowy, but the whites of their eyes shone out.

Andrew leaned against the wall, sweat cold on his forehead, heart hammering as though trying to burst out of his chest.

When he had the courage to look down the corridor he saw a white figure coming towards him. It was a nurse carrying a tray of medicines and a glass.

He straightened up, trying to be nonchalant. 'The eyes,' he said idiotically; 'the eyes!'

She nodded her head as though she understood, before disappearing into the dark. She must be the matron, he thought, and wondered who'd been taken ill and was in need of the medicine.

A hand clamped down on his shoulder. He shouted out as he whirled round to find himself staring into Bradshaw's grinning face.

'Were you scared, Conlan? It's only a power cut. You'll have to get used to them, lad; we have more power cuts here than hot dinners.'

Andrew turned and walked unsteadily towards his room with Bradshaw's laughter following him.

The next few days were busy ones while Andrew became familiar with the school, and then the boys arrived in a welter of noise, shouts and running feet.

He found that he enjoyed teaching and was getting on well with his pupils. At first he was worried that they might be curious about what he'd done in the war, but after two weeks nothing had been said and Andrew relaxed.

Several times he'd glimpsed the matron about the house. He'd see her at the end of the corridor or hurrying up the stairs, quiet and efficient. One day he called out to her, but she didn't stop or wait for him to catch up.

Three weeks into the term found Andrew standing beside the football pitch cheering on St Anthony's against a tough local team.

At half-time Andrew walked over to encourage the boys, some of whom were in his class. They were gathered round Bradshaw, who was haranguing them about being pathetic softies letting the opposition run rings round them. When he saw Andrew approaching he raised his voice: 'Well, well, here comes our conquering hero. No need to worry any more, gentlemen, Mr Conlan will set you straight. He's no shrinking violet seeing ghosties in the dark!'

Someone giggled, and Andrew saw that it was Parker, a boy in his class.

'That's right, lads, you ask Mr Conlan what he did in the war. He'll tell you how to be tough.'

At that moment the umpire's whistle blew and the boys scattered back to the field. Bradshaw brought his face close to Andrew's so that he could smell the rank sweat and bad breath.

'You tell 'em, pretty boy.'

Andrew watched him follow the boys and felt sick.

That night he couldn't sleep. He went over and over the confrontation with Bradshaw. He was sure that he knew about his history and wondered if Marsden had been indiscreet. Parker, too, was on his mind. The boy had stared at him during supper and whispered something to the others, then they'd all looked at Andrew, smirking and giggling.

He punched his pillow and closed his eyes, but it was no good; sleep was far away. He finally got up and made some tea. He drank it, looking out of his window towards the cliffs and sea. The clouds were moving quickly over the pale sky. He could hear the distant boom of the sea breaking on the rocks.

He was turning away when his eye was caught by a shifting of shadows. His breathing quickened. Surely it couldn't be …? He stared intently. Yes, it was her, matron.

She had her back to him, staring out to sea, motionless, even her clothes defying the wind as though she were frozen.

Andrew felt his heart go out to her. What was she doing? Who was she waiting for? He couldn't take his eyes off her, he hardly breathed, so intently did he watch her. Then she turned her head to the left, deliberately, as though she were aware of his gaze.

Then it came to him, she was waiting for him. She needed him, he could sense it; what a fool he was to have lingered by the window.

Fearful that she would not wait for him, he ran out of the room, along the corridor, past the watching eyes; down the stairs to the hall. He wrestled with the heavy bolts on the front door and was finally out on to the terrace.

She was still there. He ran, his feet making no sound on the damp grass. But she must have heard something for she looked over her shoulder, her face a black patch in the dim light.

'Wait,' he called, 'don't go!'

Then, in his haste, his foot was caught in tree roots and he fell heavily. Shaken, he scrambled to his feet, but she'd gone. Bewildered he walked forward looking round, searching, calling; there was no sign of her.

Andrew woke in the morning with a splitting headache. By four o'clock his headache was worse. Tea had been laid out in the staffroom where, due to rationing, he was allowed one round of sandwiches and one slice of cake. He helped himself to a cup of tea but couldn't face the salmon paste sandwiches or the grey-looking sponge cake.

'You look done in, Conlan.' It was Chivers.

'Just a headache.'

'Matron will give you some aspirin, old boy. Look, she's just come in.'

'Where?' Andrew, heart pounding, swung round.

'There!' Chivers pointed to a plump little woman dressed in a white overall.

'But … that's not her.'

'Course it is, old chap.' Chivers helped himself to extra sandwiches; if Conlan wasn't going to eat his share, then he would.

'But,' Andrew hesitated, 'does matron have an assistant?'

'No, she copes on her own; capable woman is matron.'

'Then who is the nurse?'

'What nurse?'

But they were interrupted by the school secretary, who

took Chivers off to the head's office to meet some prospective parents.

The following Sunday the whole school attended the morning service of remembrance. The church was full. Among the congregation were men from both wars wearing their medals with pride. Many people had tears in their eyes as they sang the hymns and prayed for those who would never return home. Andrew felt isolated, finding it difficult to join in the service. He hadn't fought in his war, he hadn't lost anyone dear to him; what right did he have to sit among those who had? He went through the motions like everyone else, knowing himself to be a coward and a sham.

Afterwards, he lingered in the pale sunlight, wandering among the ancient graves, reluctant to return to school. The boys would be full of it all, wanting stories of battles and escapes. The sea was a distant murmur, a horse and cart clip-clopped past while voices faded and all became quiet.

He closed his eyes and felt the soft breeze stir his hair. It was soothing, reminding him of his mother, how she used to stroke his hair to comfort him. He realised then that he, too, had lost loved ones because of the war. His refusal to fight and kill had led to estrangement between him and his parents as well as his friends. He'd suffered because of his principles and consequently endured a hard and bitter war. He wondered if he would ever see his mother again.

He opened his eyes and saw the nurse standing in front of

a grave. Her head was bent as though in prayer or mourning; again the breeze didn't disturb her nurse's cap or apron.

He found that he couldn't move, as though he'd been turned to stone. She bent down to lay something on the grave, straightened, before disappearing among the trees.

When she'd gone he felt strength returning to his limbs. He walked slowly to the grave and he saw what she'd put on it: a white feather stark on the black earth. He lifted his eyes and read the name on the headstone: 'Andrew Conlan. 1918–1946'.

He screamed. The rooks, startled out of the trees, screamed with him.

When he opened his eyes next, the rector was looking down at him. 'Where am I?' Andrew stammered.

'It's all right, you're in my study. We've phoned the school and they're sending someone for you.'

'I saw … I saw my name on the grave and … and …'

'And what?'

'Nothing!' Andrew couldn't bring himself to mention the white feather. 'I saw my name. It was my name.' He began to cry with deep, wrenching sobs.

'Mr Conlan,' said the rector, patting his shoulder, 'it wasn't your name on the grave, believe me, it wasn't.' He handed Andrew a large handkerchief. 'Here you are, you don't want your headmaster to see you like this. If you feel up to it I can take you outside and prove that the grave doesn't have your name on it.' There was a pause while Andrew wiped his eyes and blew his nose. 'You see,' the rector continued, 'the name on the grave is Arthur Carstairs, and I believe that your eye caught the two initials A and C, which are the same as yours. The brain often plays tricks, especially if we're not feeling well. I believe that you'll feel better if you can pluck up courage to look at poor Arthur's grave.'

Andrew allowed himself to be led out into the churchyard once more.

'There now, you can see for yourself. "Arthur Carstairs. 1888–1917". His was a sad story: poor chap was a conscientious objector in the First War. He went through a bad time, spent over a year in prison. He had a sister, a nurse, who spent most of the war at the front. When she came home on leave she tried to make him join up but he wouldn't. He was a gentle man, a bit simple, couldn't bear the thought of killing another human being. Are you all right, Mr Conlan?'

'Yes.'

'I shouldn't have brought you out in the cold, I'm sorry.'

'It's all right. What happened to him?'

'Every time he saw his sister she'd give him a white feather, making sure it was in public and humiliating. She stirred up a lot of hatred against Arthur.'

The two men stood in silence at the foot of the grave.

The vicar spoke softly. 'He was found at the bottom of the cliffs. Some said he'd jumped deliberately, others made out it was an accident. We'll never know the truth of it.'

But Andrew knew. 'What happened to the sister?'

'She went back to France and died there.'

That night, back in his room, he waited for her. He kept watch through the window but she didn't appear in the garden; this time she came up behind him. He saw her reflection in the glass, gliding without a sound towards him, holding something in her hand. He turned to face her and she held out the white feather. Her face in the moonlight was white; everything about her was starched, white and implacable. She was very close to him now and he could smell the sickly scent of rotting flowers.

⋆⊸◉ ◉⊷⋆

They called for the rector very early next morning.

Marsden told him they'd heard a terrible cry and the sound of breaking glass. 'It was an accident of course, a real tragedy.'

They stood looking down at the broken body of Andrew Conlan.

'You've sent for the police?' said the rector.

'Yes, though it's a straightforward situation. He obviously couldn't sleep, wanted some fresh air, and fell. He was a bit of a nervy chap you know.' Marsden fell silent, then muttered, 'Damn war.'

'There'll have to be an inquest.'

'Of course.' Marsden thought of all the unwelcome publicity.

The rector was about to say a prayer when he noticed something clutched in the dead man's hand.

'What's that?' he asked.

The two men bent closer. It was a single white feather.

WATER TAXI BACCOO

David G. Gibson

STANDING IN THE SURF waiting for a break in the rollers, Leroy felt the gooseflesh begin to tingle on his skin. Launching his dinghy into the swell, he glanced up at the sky, searching for an omen to explain his uneasiness, but saw nothing more threatening than a few wisps of cloud pegged above the listless manchineel trees and coconut palms. The trees along the strand offered a landmark to returning fishermen; not that he'd need that any more, he reflected bitterly. When his hand became snagged in a net and got dragged into the winch, it put paid to his fishing exploits for good.

He worked the single oar at the stern with his good hand, unable to shake off his strange sense of foreboding. Maybe too much rum last night, or that toke of ganja had been stronger than he'd supposed? Reaching his mooring, he secured the dinghy, transferred two jerry cans of fuel aboard the unglamorous water taxi that now offered him a livelihood and clambered aboard.

'Sure ain't no fishing boat,' he had complained to his wife after his first day. 'She nothin' more than a raft wit' two Yamahas at one end and a canopy made of fishing net.'

'You jus' be thankful you still here,' Yvette had scolded. 'Everybody know de sea ain't got no back door.'

After topping up the fuel tanks in the stern, he subjected the blue matting that covered the deck to close scrutiny. It had become an obsession with him to keep the matting clear of sand. He had gone so far as to install a basin of sea water at the top of the entry ramp, insisting that all passengers boarding from the beaches first remove their footwear and rinse their feet in the basin. It was his way of asserting himself over all those well-heeled customers who made use of his taxi.

A burst of static came from the radio. Pre-tuned out of habit to channel sixteen, the local fishing wavelength, he recognised the call sign of old Sylvester, his former fishing partner, and bent closer to glean what he could from the sporadic chatter.

'Dis here de *Hibiscus* outa Speightstown ... we lying 'bout twelve mile due west ... fish be jumpin' all over we, but pressure be fallin' ... squall maybe headin' inshore ... *Hibiscus* out.'

Leroy frowned at the predicted weather change. Surely the

wrong time of year for a squall? Still troubled, he brought the ungainly craft in through the breakers, expertly judging the right moment to let the waves nudge her ashore, then using the engines to hold her against the undertow. Only then could he use the winch to lower the twin ramps, right-hand one for entry, left-hand for exit.

The water taxi offered a service to a consortium of four hotels along a stretch of waterfront known as the Platinum Coast, allowing guests to share their facilities. There was the usual cluster of passengers on the strand in front of the Tamarind Cove Hotel. Most of them seemed to know the drill. They stood barefoot on the sand, footwear dutifully in hand, waiting to board. Leroy permitted himself a secret smile, until he spotted one child still wearing sandals in his father's arms.

'Mind de sand in him shoes,' he bellowed.

The embarrassed father obliged while Leroy smugly kept up the show of supervising the ritual rinsing of feet before allowing each individual to step aboard. Only then would he ease the throttle to half-astern and gently draw his craft into deeper water.

As he swung the cumbersome vessel on to a bearing for Coconut Creek, he spotted a hunched figure astride a jet ski tearing straight towards him out of the morning sun.

'Wha' in de worl'?'

The words froze on Leroy's lips as he desperately spun the

wheel in what had to be a futile attempt to avoid a collision. At the last possible moment, the dreadlocked rider throttled back and put the jet ski into a steep banking turn that brought it to an abrupt standstill at the expense of drenching some of the nearside passengers in spray.

Leaning over the rail to remonstrate, Leroy was astonished to see the grinning miscreant heave a knapsack towards him. It sailed narrowly passed his ear and landed heavily on the deck with a crunch of breaking glass.

'Yuh forgot yuh lunch, ol' man,' the Rasta figure called. 'Yvette say yuh forget yuh head soon.'

Leroy angrily squinted into the glare. He could not make out the rider clearly, but he appeared to have a strangely wizened face on his young shoulders. 'Ma wife sure ain't any of yuh bizness,' he called, 'whoever y'ah.'

With an insolent wave, the figure roared off, already lost behind the venting plume of water, his peals of laughter echoing eerily across the bay.

'Wussless vagabond,' Leroy growled. 'Ain't got no respec'.'

He tried to dismiss the youth as just another of the tearaways who roared up and down the shoreline touting for custom among the tourists with money to burn, but he could not. For one thing something strange had come over his passengers. He would have expected them to be jabbering among themselves at the shenanigans of the insolent youth, but instead they seemed strangely subdued. As he edged into

Coconut Creek, his passengers began to push towards the exit ramp as if in a hurry. Stranger still, no further passengers were waiting to come on board. That was a first. He recalled an old Bajan saying: 'When hogs dance, look fuh rain.'

He rummaged in his knapsack. Sure enough, his water bottle had been smashed, its contents long since leaked into the fabric. Mercifully, his lunch was protected from a soaking. With no alternative, he prepared to back out and head for his next port of call. Looping the nylon line round the small capstan on the console, he engaged the gearing and slowly raised the ramps like a drawbridge, at the same time easing the cumbersome vessel away from the shore.

Turning to check that his seaway was clear, he spotted the set of sandy footprints trailing all the way to the stern. Then he became aware of the sudden drop in temperature, and his gooseflesh returned with a vengeance. 'In de name …'

The words choked in his throat.

The apparition sat sprawled in a seat; its eyes shining with the luminosity of obsidian. Superficially, it looked like the tearaway who had roared up earlier, but a closer look made his blood run cold. This was no flesh and blood rasta. This … this duppy seemed to lack any blood at all. Then he remembered the broken water bottle and it came to him. This was no ordinary duppy, this was the legendary baccoo! He had first heard of it on his grandmother's knee. Baccoos lived in bottles and had the power to do good or evil. Feverishly he tried to remember more but, his mind in turmoil, he could not concentrate.

'Was de matter, ol' man, cat got ya tongue?'

That gave Leroy another jolt. The voice sounded exactly like Sylvester's. His throat felt dry. He could have used a swig of the lost water. With an effort, he tried to pretend everything was normal, then perhaps the baccoo would just leave him be. He gestured at the empty chairs. 'Need to get on,' he said. 'Passengers waitin'.'

The baccoo shook its head. 'Be no more passengers today, Leroy. We all two goin' fishin'.'

'But ...' Leroy wanted to protest that the water taxi was not equipped for the rougher waters of the fishing grounds, quite apart from a lack of fishing gear, but the words wouldn't come as the insolent eyes glinted darkly.

'Cool out, man,' it said. 'Bes' do as ah say.'

Lacking the will to resist, Leroy turned the taxi towards open water. The one good thing was he no longer had to look the baccoo in the eye. Instead, he faced a darkening sky. Out beyond the reef, great sails of black rain clouds swept towards them like some marauding pirate vessel. The air the wind drove before it was heavy with the smell of brimstone while the sea had turned a muddy brown.

'Ya doin' right by Yvette?' the spirit asked.

Leroy jumped at the mention of his wife. 'Do ma best,' he muttered.

'And yuh daughter, Sharon? High time dat girl be tyin' de knot. Cut pumpkin don' keep.' Leroy squirmed. How in hell did this malevolent spirit know so much about him? Despite the chill in the air, he felt himself break into a sweat. Surreptitiously, he reached for the half-bottle of rum he kept under the console for small emergencies. It had never been more sorely needed. Unscrewing the cap he took a quick gulp. The liquid burned its way down his throat.

'Some o dat fuh me?' the baccoo said.

Leroy meekly handed over the bottle. A moment later, he heard a revolting series of slurping sounds behind him.

The water taxi was hopeless in rough seas at the best of times. Out of the lee of the island's land mass, it could only be a matter of time before they were swamped by waves whipped up by the south-easterly trades. Bizarrely, though, the sea settled into a sluggish rhythm as long compact waves slid foamlessly beneath the hull. His precious blue carpet was, however, awash and the wind began gusting alarmingly.

'Time ta drop yuh net,' the ghostly figure ordered.

Leroy tried to protest that he had no net, but the baccoo merely pointed a long bony finger at the overhead canopy. While Leroy hacked it down with his knife, the spirit gestured at two young palm trees neatly tied with strong twine and stowed behind the back row of seating. Some passenger in a panic to get off must have left them behind. Leroy cut some of the fronds and awkwardly lashed them to the end floats.

In the heavy swell, he had to struggle to pay out his improvised net – some forty yards of it. Hunching down to wait, he shivered wretchedly as the wind tugged and pulled and jostled him, while the rain seeded the gusts like cold shrapnel. This could only end badly, he thought. Either the baccoo would kill him or he would perish at sea.

'Anyting to eat?' the baccoo demanded. Remembering he had not yet eaten the kingfish and conkies Yvette had prepared for him, Leroy submissively handed over the food wrapped in its steamed banana leaves. The baccoo wasted no time in sampling the traditional fare.

'Mmn, dis kingfish be good.' The baccoo raised the parcel of food to his nose and sniffed appreciatively. 'Jus' brimmin' wit' flavour an' spices.' He took a bite and more sounds of pleasure escaped from his bloodless lips. Leroy felt himself salivate at the thought of all that cornmeal, coconut, pumpkin, sweet potato and raisins being guzzled by the creature. His empty stomach rumbled as the baccoo continued to torment him. 'Ol' man,' it said. 'Dis here food be heaven on earth.'

Rising to the surface the fish began to burst from the water around them. Extending their pectoral fins like wings, they seemed to glide over the water, sometimes for as much as thirty metres. Leroy found himself wishing with all his heart that he could be free like them, but some soared straight into the net. Others, seeking the shade of the giant fronds, became entangled in the mesh beneath.

'Enough,' the baccoo abruptly called. 'Time ta haul in.'

Leroy struggled to attach one end of the net to his small winch. He was doubtful if it would stand the strain of a full net. At first it seemed to do the job but, as the net became heavier with fish, it began to squeal in protest and emit ominous puffs of blue smoke.

He tried to use his good hand to ease the tension as veins of lightning began to flare and pulse behind the clouds, turning the bruised sky a deep red like arterial blood pulsing through capillaries.

Momentarily distracted, Leroy's good hand became entangled in the mesh. The winch kept tightening the net around it. 'Not again!' he cried.

'Only one ting to do.' Out of the corner of his eye, Leroy saw the baccoo approach, a knife raised above its head.

The winch gave another jerk and Leroy passed out.

⇥ ⇤

'Ahoy there. Ahoy!' The voice seemed to come from far off.

Leroy gave a start and discovered the *Hibiscus* drawn up alongside. On his knees, but seemingly alone aboard the water taxi, he could see his own bewilderment reflected in Sylvester's eyes.

'Whassup?' Leroy said.

Sylvester tutted. 'Yuh got passengers waitin'.'

'Huh? Time is it?'

'Time yuh stopped fussin' over dat matting and started workin',' Sylvester said.

Leroy shook his head. 'Wus fixin' the overhead canopy,' he said. 'Musta had a dizzy spell is all.'

Sylvester glanced pointedly at the empty rum bottle on the deck and shook his head.

'T'ought maybe he had his hooks in yuh.'

'Who?'

'Dat ol' baccoo, dat who.'

Leroy shivered as the rest of the legend came back to him. One found good or evil, prosperity or disaster in baccoos according to how they were treated. He glanced at the blue matting under his feet and the cloudless blue sky overhead and a hesitant smile flickered across his face. 'In yuh dreams, man,' he said rather unconvincingly. Then, more assertively, 'In yuh dreams.'

As he stooped to pick up the rum bottle to throw it over the side, he noticed the blue matting glistening in rainbow hues. Going down on one knee, he discovered a myriad fish scales refracting the sunlight.

Slowly, Leroy felt the gooseflesh begin to tingle on his skin.

SEA LEGS

Linda Oliver

THE HISS AND THUD OF HYDRAULICS squeezing shut
the doors behind him signalled the departure of the bus and
awakened a general anxiety; he was under his own steam now
and two miles away from the sanctuary of his home.

When there had been two of them to make this weekly
sortie to the shops it had been an outing, something to make
an effort for: shoes polished the night before; a touch of
lipstick and powder and a colourful scarf for Meggie. Looking
out for each other, they had been relaxed and had noted aloud
the changes since their last visit – another till in the greengrocer's, James, he must be doing well. Other observations
would be tucked away to furnish their conversation for the
rest of the week – did you notice the church is almost done?
All that blackness sanded away.

Shopping alone was a chore and a trial. Would he remember to pay the electricity bill? It was not a weekly task, so likely to be forgotten. Would he manage the weight of his bag without a muscle seizing up? Though he had lived near the sea all his life, once the bus had heaved itself away, the impulse to turn and gaze on the seascape that would confront him was as irresistible as ever. He looked at the broad, sullen swell of unbroken waves, dark and threatening as black ice on tarmac, but today it made his spirits sag further. As he turned towards the shops, he was startled by the swift approach of a child.

The child, all in pink, threading her way along the pavement on a shiny scooter, briefly threatened his balance, but she was too involved in her game to even notice the slight, tidily dressed man clutching his walking stick. The fear of falling dried his mouth, and he thought ahead to the cup of milky coffee he would enjoy later. He always flinched when first hearing the roar of the gadgetry behind the café counter, but he would be able to check his list, gather his wits, and stretch his feet before standing at the bus stop.

First though, he made his way around the three narrow terraces of small shops, from the butcher's to the cheese shop to the greengrocer, missing out the ice-cream parlour, the pottery and sundry other day-tripper haunts. The chocolate-box selection of local retailers showed the council had been picky on its taxpayers' behalf. Pawnbroker, bookmaker and tattooist were conspicuous by their absence. Quaint cursive signs over bull's-eye-paned windows told visitors that old-fashioned courtesy had counted here long before the recent slew of Health, Safety and Equality acts had written civility into civil law.

At the end of the first row was a small library, where he had been an assistant for many years, and where he and Meggie had been among the chief mainstays of the Tuesday Book Club. He would save the library visit for another day. He had a sense that Meggie was disappointed by that decision and rebuked himself for such a foolish thought.

James paused for breath, resting his bag on a step, and took in the window display before him. 'Eileen's Boutique,' said the sign, and then smaller, underneath, 'prop. Jane Smith'. Neo-crimplene separates, nautically themed, with just a smattering of red, said: nothing to be afraid of here; we are affordable and we don't stop at size sixteen. Meggie had had some nice things from here. He wondered why he'd never asked her who Eileen was. He could almost feel Meggie's comfortable presence beside him, and had a sense that there was something important that she wanted him to know, but it had nothing to do with the identity of Eileen.

After his coffee, with no lavatory convenient, he hurried, head down and too fast for comfort, across the busy road to the Crab Arms, whose 'gents' was just through its side door. He remembered the days when he had the bladder of a town planner and didn't have to resort to such furtive activity.

Once at the bus stop, laden with a solid fresh loaf, local cheese and sausages, and an organically grown cauliflower, he lowered the bag to the ground, straightening up stiffly with a little puff of relief. When bending his back and using a spade had required no thought and little effort, he had grown his own vegetables in his small back garden.

Meggie had enjoyed their ritual of counting the green beans every morning until they amounted to a boiling, and together they had selected the best cauliflower for Sunday dinner. She had watched its cutting and trimming with loving pride, as if he had slain a wild beast for their table. With sprigs of the greenest mint shoots nipped off for mint sauce, they would return to their kitchen, where Meggie would plunge the vegetables in salted water and wait with gritted teeth for the hidden slugs to float off them. She would chop the mint leaves with a heavy bone-handled carving knife; he could picture her yellow, sap-stained hands. Later, he would open the oven door carefully, standing back as the aromas of sweet vinegary mint sauce and roast lamb fused in a blast of hot, crackling air. He was so absorbed in wistfully savouring this gift of a memory, that at first he didn't notice the commotion outside the Au Lait café.

Two women appeared to be comforting an all-in-pink little girl, who was upset and wailing – no other word for it – for her mother. She was pointing down the hill after a young woman – it did look like a slim woman in jeans – who was running away from the scene. The café proprietor, looking put out, took the girl by the hand and gently led her to the ice-cream freezer by the door. The women were now turned to where the jeans-clad figure had disappeared from his view; both faces expressed disgusted disbelief. James was amused to find himself mentally referring to the research presented in last weekend's paper on the 21 distinct expressions a human face can wear. Though, if he was honest, he thought most people could recognise the disgusted disbelief look before it became someone's PhD fodder. His curiosity was piqued, but was not to be satisfied, as the arrival of the bus brought him sharply back to his own concerns.

A stench of diesel fumes pinched his sinuses painfully and, already feeling nauseous, he braced himself to endure the stale air inside. Once aboard, he was anxious to sit down before the bus lurched into motion. As he sidled into the window seat on the front row, a young man swung himself, at the last moment, on to the platform, all energy and laughter. He greeted the driver as if they were acquaintances, and perched himself on the edge of the empty front seat, leaning forward, eager to talk to him.

'That lass Morag,' he started. 'You'll never believe what she's done.' He paused to allow the driver to show some interest. 'She nicks a woman's purse in the café, but she's been seen, so she legs it, don't she. Forgetting, like, that she's only got her little 'un a yard behind her.' He guessed his listener could see where this was going. 'Yep. She just left her there.' Having told the bones of his story, he repeated it and commiserated with the child's lot, until the driver waved him off at his stop and then turned the engine off. The bus was running slightly early, and this was the best spot to kill a couple of minutes and sort his small change.

So, thought James, that was what it had all been about. A sudden rush of unbearable sadness washed over him, leaving him cold and shaking. Not because of the plight of the child, most likely already reunited with her mother, but because, even though he could clearly imagine the exchange they would have had, there was no Meggie to shake her head with him and, ultimately, to see the humour in the bolting purse snatcher's predicament. He looked around, feeling that the rawness of his pain must have been visible to his fellow passengers, and then he made a conscious effort to push back thoughts of Meggie. He turned his head to the view from the coast road, where the solid leaden waves of earlier had taken on a new complexion.

Sky and sea presented a shimmering band of opalescent light in which he could faintly detect a horizon. The shore here was close to the road and just now it was unpeopled, with the exception of the young captain of a single canoe. Wearing only shorts, he was standing upright and punting his craft across the still, milky bay. In the pearly light, he made the English scene look delicately exotic, even mystical. He could have been on the Nile or the Ganges or navigating a Venetian lagoon. As James watched the hypnotic progress of the gondolier, he was soothed by it, but the glittering light made his eyes water. He was sorry that when he blinked away the tears in his eyes, it seemed that he had blinked away the boy, too. But the challenges of his trip were almost over, and he began to look forward to the company of his collie, Bess, and found that he had an appetite for the sausage supper he was planning.

A short time later he alighted; he waited until the bus had groaned its way through the gear changes that got it on its way, and then filled his nostrils with clean air. The perfumes of wild lilac and Virginia stocks, released by the warmth of the afternoon, told him he was home. As he turned in at his own garden gate, he was glad to hear the metallic click of the latch behind him, a sound that he had been hearing for half a lifetime. His kitten-faced pansies needed water, he thought.

Leaving a neighbouring house, only feet away, was Stan. The two men passed the time of day, and Stan listened to the story of 'that Morag'. 'Three bairns left in a café,' said Stan. 'Priceless.'

'Only one child,' James reminded him.

'Not when I tell it down the Legion,' said Stan, laughing and winking as he went, amused by his own wit.

When James laughed too, he was shocked by how unfamiliar the sound of his own laughter had become to him.

Claws skittered urgently on tiles behind his front door, and a tail was wagging so hard it was thwacking the bottom stair, so he opened the door wide for Bess to escape her prison, and her uncontainable woofs cheered his homecoming. Safe from flying dogs, James supported himself on the hallstand with one hand and stooped to pick up his local paper. He stroked an old scar in the cool grain of the oak that had been polished so often it seemed almost to be healed. The idea came to him then that he was like the boy balanced in his canoe.

We are at opposite ends of the same journey, he reflected. He holds up his head and is drawn forward towards his destination, or even his destiny, but he is connected to the present. Through the soles of his feet and the muscles of his body, he feels the dips and rolls of the water, and its currents are forces that challenge him right now. This was book club territory, but he knew this train of thought was serious. Although it is my past that charges my spirit, I, too, am borne on present tides, whose unexpected eddies excite my course. Willpower is what keeps both of us afloat and neither of us must give in. He breathed in deeply. Meggie was behind this moment of insight, he thought, unreasonably, but with absolute certainty.

As he held the newspaper at arm's length to scan its front page, he thought the word 'canoe' in the headline was one of those coincidences that are a million to one chance. Once, he had switched TV channels and two completely different programmes had used the word 'tulip' in the space of four seconds. But the hairs on his arms stood up and the back of his neck tingled as he walked to the kitchen and sat down to read.

The story, from ten miles along the coast, of a birdwatcher who had seen a young man leap from a canoe to rescue a floundering swimmer, rooted him to the chair. He read how the witness claimed to have seen the man pulling the young woman on to a sand dune, but when he reached her, only minutes later, she was alone and told him she had made her own way ashore. Scrutiny of the sea and the dunes through his powerful binoculars had revealed only a distant white sail and a score of bobbing gulls. The newspaper valued its credibility and took the line of praising the bravery of the shy rescuer.

James pictured the still silhouette of the boy. He understood that he had been rescued, just as the woman had been saved, when she was desperately seeking the sandy ridges beneath her feet. And, as he wondered if it was a fleeting tang of sweet mint sauce he could catch in the air, he smiled. This would not be a tale he would share with Stan and his Legionnaires, but he knew what he knew. He put aside the newspaper and flicked the switch on his kettle, and then he reminded himself that, after supper, the pansies should have some water.

ALDGATE ECHOES

Lucy Brown

LONDON WAS NEVER VOICELESS. Not like this.

The square I'd taken refuge in would be a crowded smoking area come tomorrow morning. But, tonight, every agitation that occupied it during the day was lost beneath the spongy mist settling over the city. A haphazard arrangement of oblong stone benches and an assortment of statuesque and squat buildings littered the pavement with shadows cast from the flickering streetlamps. A corner surrounding one ugly skyscraper was boxed off by gigantic blue boards. A door was visible within one, wedged partly open by a vodka bottle.

I heard footsteps further down the alley, towards the road I'd fled from. Blood still clung to my arm, drying and flaking off as I shivered. They'd stolen my jacket when I'd refused to give them my bag without a fight. One of them had thrown me to the ground as they fled. But there was nothing to say they wouldn't come back. I shook harder as I listened for further noises.

They came in the form of scuffling and a rasping cough. I let out an involuntary whimper and the area stilled.

Then he called, 'Is someone down there?'

He was old. Well, older than my muggers at least. But that didn't make him any less of a threat. I waited and prayed he'd turn away but he didn't. The footsteps came closer and I had to act. Rushing towards the door in the construction boards, I lunged against it with my bad arm. It was jammed from the other side but I'd gained enough momentum to force my way through it.

I pressed my back against the filthy boards and willed myself into absolute silence, something I was unused to. The gaping hole was still visible from the square but I hoped the shadows would hide me. From the alley came the lumbering figure of a man in his fifties or thereabouts. He was a guard somewhere; he wore the same bland uniform as everyone else on the night shift. I thought of Jeremy and his cosy hut right now. He thought I was safe at home.

After a brief look around the man muttered to himself and returned the way he'd come. I released my breath and finally took in my surroundings.

There was debris scattered around the base of the building – bricks and smashed light-bulbs with strips of wood littered around for good measure. A chunky skip was situated off to the left, beside the glass entrance which had been shattered from the outside. I wasn't stupid enough to venture inside so I edged towards my slender exit.

Then a voice from the shadows struck me cold.

'Don't go.'

Remaining motionless, I tried to place the childlike tones in the context of my own head. I was scared – petrified even. Of course, I was hearing things. I needed to get to the police, get to Jeremy before …

'Please don't go. I'm scared here on my own.'

My head felt removed from my body. The latter was turning when I was pleading with it to stop. Nevertheless, I found my eyes returning to the hitherto empty doorway that led into the building. Stood on the top step was a young boy, perhaps seven or eight, dressed warmly in a tracksuit and wearing an orange bobble hat. Little square glasses were perched on his nose, obscuring the plaintive look in his eyes until he lifted his chin.

'W-what are you doing out here on your own?' I asked, trying to be the adult I was. 'It's almost three in the morning.'

'I got scared,' he said simply. His voice was matter-of-fact, as if he was reeling off the results of some scientific test. That was the kind of boy he was; I understood that in an instant. Laconically scratching his ear, he added, 'There were these men chasing me. I came in here because it looked safe. So they couldn't follow me.'

I let out my breath. For some reason encountering a kid in the madness of the evening didn't panic me as much as it would've usually. The normal me would've rushed him to the closest police station, or at least insisted he call his parents. But it wasn't like I had my mobile phone anyway.

'I've had a little fight tonight as well,' I said, holding up my arm for demonstration. 'What's your name?'

'Toby.'

'I'm Angie, nice to meet you.'

He smiled widely. 'So I haven't scared you?'

'A bit, but that's what happens when you sit in old buildings. Do you live near here?'

'I'm visiting my nan; she lives in Bethnal Green. But she won't have noticed I'm not there, don't worry. She always falls asleep about eight o'clock. Leaves the door wide open and I wanted to see the fair tonight.'

I must've been out of touch; I hadn't heard of anything. 'There was a fair tonight?'

'In Leicester Square. It was amazing. Huge rides to make your eyes pop out. I stood on my tiptoes to get on the big one.'

'And did you manage it?' I questioned.

'Yep,' he said proudly, then the grin slipped from his face. 'But then I was walking back to the tube station and these lads saw me. Started picking on me. I ran away and I came here. What time is it, please?'

His sudden seriousness surprised me. 'Three minutes past three,' I replied after checking my watch. 'Why?'

'I think I have to go soon, that's all.'

'Well, I'll get you home,' I said decisively. 'Don't know about you but I could do with some company on the way back. We can look after each other.'

This time his smile was faint. 'Okay.'

'What's wrong?' I asked. 'Don't you want to go home?'

'I think they'll all be mad at me. I shouldn't have snuck out like that.'

'Well, no, but I'm sure they'll just be happy you're all right. I mean, look at me. You could've been hurt out here tonight.'

I was growing a little impatient. The adrenalin rush from the chase had completely evaporated into the chilly air now. I was shivering uncontrollably and envying him his woolly tracksuit. The boards all around kept me out of a direct draught, but the iciness seemed to be sweeping through the very brickwork of the building in front of me. I wondered if he'd consider sharing his bobble hat on the walk to the police station.

'You're lucky,' he said abruptly.

'Am I?' I chuckled drily. 'I don't feel it right now. I feel like someone threw me into the road and tried to kick my guts out. Actually, that's very nearly what happened. God, I shouldn't be telling you this, you're only a kid.'

His face was expressionless. 'That's what my family always say but it doesn't mean I don't understand.'

'Very wise,' I conceded. 'Now, be a bit wiser and come with me. Let's get home before dawn if we can. Then your nan might not be so mad.'

'Oh, she will be,' he said with certainty. 'She'll be fuming.'

'I'll try explaining it to her,' I promised. 'Toby, come on. Please. I'm cold.'

Now he was looking past me. 'Do you hear that?'

Instantly, I turned to the gap I'd slid through but everything beyond it was silent. When I looked back, Toby had disappeared into the building. I heard his footsteps clattering up some stairs, reverberating for what felt like minutes. My first thought was that he was retrieving whatever he'd brought out with him. For a while I waited tolerantly, then I heard a noise above my head.

Craning my neck, I almost stopped breathing. There was Toby – on a ledge about six floors up.

It was a thin thing, barely able to take his weight by the look of it. He was perched with his left foot in front of his right, arms outstretched to the window.

'No, don't,' he was saying, 'please, don't.'

'Toby!' I shouted, my voice bouncing around the square like a stray bullet. 'What are you doing? Come down!'

He made no sign he'd heard me. He was still pleading with someone I couldn't see. Was it possible he'd disturbed someone else in the building, a tramp maybe? Just as I'd resolved to rush in there and find out, I heard an agonising wail.

Raising my eyes, I saw him begin to fall. His left foot buckled before his right; his knee cracked on the ledge and there was a moment when he regained his precarious balance. But he drifted right, swaying in time to some inaudible music. He was directly above the skip as his legs dislodged and he took flight.

My scream was lost in what happened next.

His body jerked upwards; not towards the ledge but upwards, over the constraints of the boards. He was translucent – all except the bobble hat. As I watched, horror-stricken, the hat slid away and fell with alarming speed into the skip beside me.

My eyes, naturally attracted to the falling object, groped their way back to the grey sky by degrees. I don't know what I expected to see, but it wasn't there. Nothing was.

The board being forced aside startled me. I leapt back in panic as a head popped through the gap. After a moment I recognised the ageing security guard.

'Bloody hell, love, you gave me a shock with that scream of yours,' he said congenially. 'Thought someone was being butchered. Are you the one what was mugged, by any chance?'

I stared at him.

His frown deepened into his wrinkles. 'There was a witness, you see. The police are out looking for you since they found blood on the road. Looks like it was from your arm, doesn't it?'

I nodded mutely.

'Come on,' he said briskly, 'let's get you out of the cold.'

He backed away to let me out. As soon as his whiskers were out of my sight I turned and grabbed the sides of the skip. The icy metal stung my arms but I barely noticed. I hoisted myself up and gazed into a pile of rubbish.

Nothing else.

It had fallen in. I knew it had. I'd watched it with my own eyes.

There was a siren in the distance. I dropped down and followed the guard out on to the square. He was lounging on a stone bench.

'Mind if I smoke?' he asked.

I just shook my head.

→━◉ ◉━←

A week later I sat on the floor with my back pressed flat against the side of the skip. I was perfectly in view of the doorway and in range of the exit. My hands were clasped around a thermos that had been emptied long since. Even through the woolly gloves I was shivering uncontrollably.

I checked my watch – almost three o'clock.

'Did I scare you?' a voice asked softly.

My involuntary shudder was superseded by relief. 'Only when I thought I'd made you up,' I replied as I stood. There was a satisfied smile on his face. 'What?'

'Nothing. Did you visit my grave?'

'Mmm. They've made it look nice.'

He touched his hat. 'I know.'

'Right, Toby,' I said with a firmness I didn't feel, 'you've got just seven minutes to tell me everything.'

'Or you could come back tomorrow,' he said hopefully.

'Or I could come back tomorrow.'

THE LAST FRIDAY IN NOVEMBER

Margaret Davies

THE LAST BUS MADE ITS WAY out of town, past rows of shop windows, now mostly in darkness, out into the country-side, along lanes that wound across the moor to the villages on its route.

There were maybe a dozen passengers, sitting hunched in their seats, lost in their thoughts or looking out of the rain-spotted windows, seeing blackness or their own reflections. Holly hadn't been on this bus since – she couldn't remember when. She usually got a lift with her dad or one of the neighbours in her village who also worked in town. When she worked the late shift at the restaurant, her boss, Greg, would take her home. Tonight he'd been called away mid-evening and she had no choice but to hurry for the last bus. Her village, Lutterby, was the last on the route, so she closed her eyes and tried to shut out the gloomy scene around her.

The bus's wheels hissed along the lonely roads, now under the half-unleaved branches of late November, now passing fields in various shades of darkness. The occasional light in an isolated house or cottage accentuated the sense of being nowhere. At each stop, the bus clattered to a halt, the doors folded open like broken wings, while passengers alighted and vanished into quiet streets.

There was little traffic to slow them down, but the journey seemed to be going on for ever. Holly yawned and sighed as the bus pulled into Bournton and stopped to deliver an elderly couple. Holly hadn't been there for years, but now remembered how, as a teenager, she had come here every Friday to the youth club at the village hall. She smiled to herself at memories of those evenings with the crowd, a mad lot, game for anything.

One night they'd danced round the village singing the chicken song, while Milly, the poor youth worker, besought them to keep quiet or the local residents would complain.

Holly felt old remembering those days. 'I'm only twenty-three,' she told herself, but the time seemed so distant and carefree. And yet there had been worries: were her clothes right? Her hair? What were her friends saying? She'd been thrilled at her relationship with Jack, her first real boyfriend, and terrified of losing him. One of the other girls had tried to take him away, but Holly and her best friend Carly had seen her off. Though the girl had been a bit of a loser, not a real threat.

The bus pulled out of Bournton and Holly left the memories behind. Not far now. They were on a lonely stretch of Moors Road, a belt of sodden trees on one side, open stretches of moorland on the other. The bus had picked up speed. Holly noticed the bus shelter ahead, but the driver had obviously decided there would be no one waiting. Who would wait at such an isolated place? There was no reason to be there.

As the bus drew alongside the shelter, Holly saw from the corner of her eye, a figure running from it to the edge of the pavement. She called out: 'There's someone at the stop.'

But the driver didn't falter. 'No, there isn't,' he said, maintaining his speed.

Holly looked back at the bus shelter. It was open on this side and she could see it was deserted. She stretched her eyes wider, trying to see again what she'd just seen: a running girl with a desperate expression on her face. There was only the emptiness of the shelter and the grass and trees around. Her face burned with embarrassment. What was it to her if there *had* been someone waiting? It was up to them to signal to the driver in time. She didn't look at the other passengers, but felt they were eyeing her warily.

By the time the bus reached Lutterby, the three remaining passengers got down, Holly the last. The other two said goodnight to the driver, but Holly didn't speak. The brusque tone in which he had contradicted her still rankled – even though he'd been right.

She let herself into the house, hoping that Greg would be back at the restaurant tomorrow and she wouldn't have to take the bus again.

⊷⊷◉ ◉⊷⊷

The memory of the journey faded and Holly did nothing to keep it alive. It had left an unpleasant sensation she was keen to shake off. She'd explained to herself that it was a reflection of a face on the bus, thrown back from the glass of the shelter. Perhaps her own face, although it had looked like – no, it didn't look like anyone she knew. A silly mistake, no need to think about it.

The evening had been busy, verging on frantic. One of the waitresses failed to show up, a table was double-booked and two large noisy parties competed for attention. Holly was run off her feet and looking forward to closing time when she carried another load of dirty dishes into the kitchen.

'Oh, by the way,' Greg said, 'I've taken the car in for its MOT. I'm staying in town with friends, but I'll make sure you get away in time for the last bus.'

Holly opened her mouth to protest, but stopped as she realised she had no choice. She couldn't afford a taxi, and Greg was obviously not offering to pay.

She hadn't thought she'd noticed the driver from the last time she'd made the journey until, seeing his long face framed by ginger sideburns, she realised it was the same man.

The passengers might also have been the same people as last time. They huddled into their seats and turned their gaze inward. In a seat by the window, near the back of the bus, Holly also withdrew into her thoughts. She resolved to switch off until the bus reached Lutterby. She looked at the date on her ticket and realised it was almost exactly a year since the last time she'd caught this bus – that had been the last Friday in November and so was this. 'I hate November,' she thought, 'each day getting darker and more miserable, Christmas still ages away.'

Despite her attempts to shut out the world, Holly was aware of the tedious journey, stopping at the usual godforsaken villages, where a few people would leave the bus and head off for their homes. At Bournton, she revived a little, remembering her teenage adventures. There was the car park where she and her friend, Carly, had – what had they been doing? She could picture them waving their arms around and chanting something. Oh yes, they'd been putting a hex on that weird girl who'd tried to take Jack away. That would teach her to steal other people's boyfriends.

Now they were on to the lonely stretch of road, where the

bus accelerated like a horse that senses its stable is nearby. The bus shelter loomed up. 'There won't be anyone there,' Holly told herself. She stared straight ahead; she wasn't going to be deluded again. Some magnetism pulled her eyes towards the shelter, and the image of the face coming towards her was so vivid that, despite herself, she cried out: 'She's there. The girl at the bus stop.'

Again the driver said curtly, 'There's no one there.' And, as if hypnotised, Holly looked back to see the empty bus shelter.

'Light reflecting on the window,' she told herself, as she shrank back in her seat. But her panicky heart refused to be calmed. The face had been so vivid, the expression anguished. 'She's only missed the bus,' Holly thought. But she hadn't missed the bus. She wasn't really there.

She got up before they reached her stop, anxious to be off the bus. But the other passengers were ahead of her and she had to wait for them to alight. She turned to look at the driver and saw that he was watching her.

He said, 'You saw her.'

'No.' Holly shook her head. 'I just thought—' Then, as the meaning of his remark penetrated, she said, 'Who is she?'

The driver drew in a long breath. He took so long to answer that Holly thought of getting off the bus. She didn't want to hear what he might say. But she couldn't move.

'Eight years ago,' the driver said, 'the last Friday in November, I was driving this bus, the last bus. It was a terrible night, the wind was howling and I was late, trying to make up for lost time. Coming along the Moors Road, the trees were blown across the way. I knew there'd be no one at the bus stop so I put my foot down. Then, as I drew alongside, she rushed out, waving frantically, but I was going too fast to stop just like that. And I thought, "Serve her right, silly cow, leaving it too late," and I kept going.'

'I don't see—' Holly began, then stopped as she saw he hadn't finished, was merely pausing to psych himself up for the next part.

'A few days later,' the driver said, 'a policeman came to the depot, wanting to know if I'd seen a girl on the Moors Road on Friday night. Seemed she'd gone missing. I said no, I hadn't seen anyone. Told myself she'd gone off with her boyfriend, the way girls do.

'Then a year later, I was driving the last bus down that road. Deserted, until I was alongside the shelter and she rushed out at me. I slammed on the brakes, but there was no one there. I looked all round, back at the shelter, on the road ahead, at the verges on either side: there was no one. I told the passengers I'd stopped because something ran across the road in front of me. Since then, I've seen her every year. No matter how hard I try to get out of it, I always end up driving this bus on the last Friday of November.'

He looked hard at Holly. 'But none of my other passengers has ever seen anything. What is she to you?'

Holly wanted to say, 'Nothing. I've no idea who she is,' but her tongue wouldn't let her. She said: 'She used to come to the youth club in Bournton. She was always a misfit. She tried to get off with my boyfriend, but he just laughed at her. Then Carly and I put a hex on her – just messing about, to warn her off. She ran away and when Carly's dad came to give us a lift home, she wasn't around. We said we didn't know where she'd got to. We told that to the police when they came asking. She must have gone off somewhere.'

In the silence that followed, Holly saw again the frightened face of the girl, running from the bus shelter. The face the driver had seen every year since she had gone missing.

Holly stepped down on to the pavement, resolving never to get that bus again. Then she remembered the driver who had made the same resolve, but was fated to repeat the journey every anniversary.

Now Holly had another reason to dread November.

NO ACCOUNTING FOR IT

Jonathan Woodmere

COLD, WET, SNOWING, PAST 1 A.M. on a Tuesday morning in the middle of April, train delayed due to signalling problems. God, who would choose to commute to the City. Twenty-five years ago it seemed exciting and certainly rewarding. Then I was just a trainee accountant, a gofer. One week in the year when I used to double my month's salary on the overtime, and eat a freebie dinner in the directors' dining room.

Now, it was my job to piece it all together, spot all the mistakes and present the annual accounts to the finance director and the chairman, and write the piece they would present to the shareholders as their own work. All right, so my salary was quintuple what I would be paid now in my old job, but I was expected to work all hours necessary – no paid overtime on my 'fat' salary. Last out of the office except for security, past midnight every day for these ten days, weekend included.

A train finally hummed, then clattered into the station. The carriage I got into was inevitably empty. I sat facing backwards, and waited another five minutes. I wish they would shut the bloody doors! They must be mind-readers: there was a hiss and they began to close, just as a man dashed across the platform, slipped as he arrived and fell forward. I didn't see his landing, but the doors opened again and he stood up instantly, apparently unharmed, and came and sat opposite to me. He was bearded, sallow and of indeterminate age, maybe mid- or late fifties, could be more. I enquired after his well-being.

'Fine,' he replied, 'probably a bruise or two. Thanks be, they have good sensors on the doors these days! Nearly squashed my head in them.'

'Just as well you caught it,' I said; 'I've been waiting fifty minutes. Signalling problems due to the weather. No telling when the next one will be.'

We each settled back in our seats, and I closed my eyes.

'... Harpenden. Harpenden next stop. This is the twelve twenty-four from St Pancras to Bedford. Please ensure ... blah, blah.' The speech penetrated my dreams, and I woke to find my fellow traveller standing and buttoning his long, old-fashioned overcoat as the train slowed.

'Thanks for your concern about my fall,' he said. 'Better luck than the poor devils in the Manchester air-crash.'

I hadn't heard of the crash. I'd heard no news today. Lunch was a sandwich on the go, our dinner brought in for us in the dining room at six in the evening. I left home at six in the morning and tonight I wouldn't be home until nearly two.

'Yes,' I vaguely replied, 'Good night.' Something about him made me feel uncomfortable, seemed slightly camp, possibly.

Part of a newspaper folded in his pocket was visible, presumably the first early edition of tomorrow's paper, and I discerned 'Horror plane cr—'.

I was glad Fiona had gone as usual to her sister's in Stockport by train this morning, and not flown from Luton. It had become customary to stay with her sister during annual report week, since she wouldn't see much of me.

In the morning, there was a sprinkling of snow on the ground as I bought a coffee and panini on the station. I was tired and, having consumed my on-the-move breakfast, I put my earphones on, listened to some Brahms and closed my eyes. Thankfully this train terminated at St Pancras, so I could sleep safely. I saw and heard no news. I rarely bothered to read, listen to or watch it these days, it was so unendingly depressing.

My week progressed as expected. That night, no ice and no rail delays. The doors on the 12.24 began to close as my bearded co-passenger of the previous night ran from the entrance and threw himself into my carriage. He sat across the aisle from me again. 'Hello. Made it safely that time!'

'Better set out a few minutes earlier next time,' I replied, putting on my headphones, signifying I had no wish for conversation.

He clearly got the message, and spoke again only as he rose when we approached Harpenden. 'Do you catch this train every night?'

I had no wish to be rude, so I gave slightly more than the monosyllabic reply his question demanded.

'Just for this week. Work commitments, it's an annual occurrence. I'm chief accountant at Frenton and Glanville.'

'Remarkable. That was my job thirty years ago. Annual budget time again, I suppose? Hope they pay you well then. Big fall on Wall Street late today. Expect London will collapse in the morning! I might catch an earlier train tomorrow. Good luck. I'm Tom Dennerston, don't suppose anyone there remembers me now. '

His folded newspaper jutted from the same coat pocket again. All I could make out of a headline was '—eet collapse spreads panic'.

Wednesday, all went quite smoothly, until Andrew, the best of my assistants, spoke to me over dinner.

'I'm sorry, Roger, but I can't be here in the morning. My brother-in-law was on the Manchester plane yesterday. We're

looking after my sister, but my wife has a hospital appointment in the morning. She must go, and I can't leave Mary
alone. I should be able to get in soon after lunch, and I'll work
through the weekend.'

I thought, 'What a bummer.'

I *said*, 'Don't worry, Andrew, we'll manage. I'm sorry I
didn't know, but I might as well ask straight out. Was your
brother-in-law killed?'

'There were no survivors, Roger. Didn't you see the news
this morning?'

'I'm so sorry, Andy. No, I didn't catch the news. Take what
time you need. We'll be grateful for any you can spare here.
Thanks for coming in for the last two days.'

I thought he looked at me a little surprisedly. Surely he
didn't think that I was so callous as to expect him to be here
in such tragic circumstances?

The 12.24 was on time again. I sat in what had become my
usual seat. It pulled out promptly, as empty as usual, no sign
even of my bearded friend tonight. I was woken by the usual
announcement approaching Harpenden. I half opened my
eyes; better not fall asleep again with just ten minutes to go. As
my stop was announced I rose and zipped up my coat. It hadn't
become much warmer outside; no more snow or ice, though.

The train jolted and threw me against the far side seat. I
noticed a newspaper lying flat on the seat, back page uppermost
with the headline, 'Two 100/1 winners at Sandown':

The last two races at Sandown yesterday produced 100/1 winners. It is believed to be the only time this has ever happened. Bookmakers reported a number of doubles on the horses in their London shops. A spokesperson for one said if no coup was detected, they would certainly pay out bets up to £10 in full. 'We were unfortunate in London name-association bets, the horses being Angel Islington and Bow Street. A £1 double paid £10,201.'

I laughed to myself. I wasn't very interested in horse racing, and had no sympathy for punters and less for bookmakers. The paper looked rather scruffy, and I let it remain on the seat as the train ground to a halt.

Thursday morning began foully, but was fine by the time we reached St Pancras. A new doorkeeper was on duty, and I had to produce my pass to get into the office.

'Mattie left us?' I enquired as he inspected it and looked me over.

'No, Mr Grindley, sir. I gather he has a day off to go to Sandown races.'

'Ah, I hope he finds some hundred to one winners then, like the two there yesterday,' I laughed.

'Wouldn't know, sir, don't follow it myself. Didn't notice a meeting at Sandown yesterday. Big crash on Wall Street, though.'

I went into my office. How odd. One of those things.

I called in Howard, who was trying to get to the bottom of a glitch we'd come across late last night. He was steadily working through the set routine, he said, implying that time spent talking to me would slow him down. Nevertheless I asked him what he knew about Roger's brother-in-law and Monday's plane crash.

'The plane crash was Tuesday morning. His wife rang and I heard him agreeing that she should fetch his sister to stay with them. They knew straight away there was no hope.'

That didn't seem quite right. Surely it was on Monday? Mind you, I was so tired from lack of sleep, my mind must be confused. I told Howard to press on and thanked him. I called my secretary, Doreen, to ask her for coffee. The doctor has warned me against drinking coffee. He diagnosed a suspected heart murmur that needs checking. I have an appointment in a fortnight's time. But I can't do without it at the moment.

Doreen is a stalwart in her sixties, been here much longer than me. The fount of all knowledge. My coffee arrived promptly, as ever. She was old-fashioned enough to know who the boss was, and to believe that men came first!

'Thanks, Doreen. Tell me, did you ever know someone called Tom, something like Denston, did my job thirty years ago?'

'You mean you don't know?'

'Sorry, don't know what?'

'His name was Dennerston. I suppose he did most of what you do. It was so, so tragic.'

'Sorry again, but what was tragic about my job?'

'I have a cutting from *The Times* in my desk. I'll fetch it and you can read it. No one here really ever speaks about it.'

A few moments later, she returned with a laminated A4 pouch, containing a cutting.

GRUESOME FIND IDENTIFIED

The head of a man, found on a northbound train when it stopped at Harpenden, has now been identified and relatives informed. The police are appealing for anyone on St Pancras Station from 11.30 p.m. on Monday night to 00.30 a.m. on Tuesday morning to come forward, especially if they boarded the 12.24 train via Harpenden. The man is now known to be Thomas Dennerston, who worked in the City and lived in Harpenden. The police have not ruled out foul play, but believe he was the victim of a tragic accident when boarding the train.

I stood up, and immediately sat down again, feeling slightly dizzy, hot and light-headed.

'Are you all right, Mr Grindley?' she said, solicitously moving my coffee a little closer.

'Yes, it's just an awful story. Did you know him?'

'I was the director's PA at the time. I saw him when he

visited the director and at meetings which I minuted. He was a nice man. It was decided at the inquest that he had probably slipped and fallen on the icy platform, rushing for the train, and his neck was trapped in the closing doors, and no one saw it happen. They found the rest of his body a few miles up the line, mostly still intact except for his foot. That was never found. Probably lucky he didn't have a wife. Some said he was ... well, you know, preferred men to women. Wasn't something you made public in those days. But I don't know and didn't care. He was a gentleman in the office. It was in all the papers.'

'Thank you, Doreen. Would you mind finding me a copy of today's *Times*, please?'

It seemed strange, and so did my fellow traveller. Odd that he fell boarding the train on Monday night. And what was that remark about having good sensors on the doors – did he say, 'These days'? Then the plane crash and the Wall Street crash: the plane crash *must* have been on Monday, because he told me about it on the first night I saw him, and it was in his paper. I went out to see Howard, ostensibly to check on progress, but really to ask him a question to put my mind at rest.

'I'm losing track of time this week, Howard. Which day did you say was the plane crash?'

'Tuesday morning. Wall Street crash yesterday afternoon. Bad week. Especially for families like Andrew's.'

'Yes. Tell him to see me when he comes in, please.'

I went back to find a copy of *The Times* on my desk. And another cup of coffee. The headline on the front page read: 'Panic in world stock markets as Wall Street crashes'. I turned to the racing page and looked at yesterday's results. None from Sandown, but I glanced at the opposite page. Sure enough there was the meeting that had attracted our doorkeeper. The last two races both seemed to have a long list of runners. I took a long drink from my coffee.

Putting my cup down, I took a deep breath and looked at the runners in the 'Maiden for 2 y.o. Fillies'. Five furlongs. Double Dutch to me. The second horse in the list was 'Angel Islington'. I shuddered before looking at the final race, similarly headed except that 'Colts' replaced 'Fillies'. Sure enough, fourth down the list was 'Bow Street'.

At lunchtime I told the office I needed some fresh air, or what passes for it in the middle of London. My colleagues were visibly surprised, I hadn't left the office at all this week.

'Just taking some exercise for half an hour.' More explanation than I needed to give them.

There were a dozen betting shops within five minutes' walk. I ventured into the first of them, belonging to a major chain. I had no idea what to expect or how to place a bet. I was surprised by the interior of the shop. A few discarded pieces of paper on the floor and surfaces, but carpeted and even a coffee machine. The walls bore neatly arranged newspaper pages from what turned out to be the *Racing Post*, and above them, banks of TV screens. I quickly spotted the paper headed 'Sandown' being pored over studiously by a short be-capped man who had a small piece of pre-printed paper on the shelf in front of him. I hoped he was helpfully inclined.

''Scuse me, but could you tell me how I put a double on two horses? Never been in a betting shop before, and the wife wants me to back two whose names she likes.'

'Sure, it's easy, tell me which they are and I'll write it for you.'

'Yes, thank you, it'll save time. They're Angel Islington and Bow Street.'

He wrote as I spoke and asked, 'Which races?'

'Oh, the 4.45 and 5.20 at Sandown.'

He showed me the betting slip and asked, 'How much do you want to put on?'

'Ten pounds.'

He looked up at me. '*Ten pounds?*'

'That's what the wife said.'

He looked behind me, at the TV screens, some of which exhibited the place and times of races and the runners. 'Jesus, mate. One's thirty-three to one and the other fifty to one. Are you sure you want to waste ten quid? Well, ask for the prices when you pay. Otherwise you'll just get starting price, and if they are going to win, they won't start at those prices!'

He handed me a neatly written ticket. Under the names

of the two horses, he had simply written '£10 double', and alongside each the time of its race.

'Thanks, didn't realise it was so easy.'

'Good luck, mate. You sure you don't know anything about them horses?'

'No, my wife had a dream.'

'Good a system as any. Perhaps I'll put 50p on.'

I handed my slip to the female cashier with a ten-pound note.

'Want the prices?'

'No, I'll just take starting price, thanks.'

'It's your funeral.' She sounded slightly sarcastic as she passed the slip through a machine and handed me a photocopy. 'Thank you, sir.'

It took fifteen minutes to visit nine more shops. Stupid, I thought, wasting my money on what must just be some sort of day-dreamed premonition. Still, a hundred pounds was less than Fiona's fare to Stockport. I tucked the receipts in my wallet, and headed back to the office where the glitch had been put right. Andrew was back. Work and dinner went on as usual. After our meal I Googled 'Results from Sandown' on my computer, and got to the *Racing Post* website. I didn't need to go to the results page. A home-page headline told me what I needed to know. My pieces of paper were worth £102,010 ... each.

A millionaire! I felt hot and dizzy again. 'Calm down,

Roger. Tomorrow, when you have collected it all, you can celebrate.'

At midnight I headed for St Pancras, pieces of paper in my wallet. The train was on time again and I sat in my usual seat, alone. We had just begun to move as my 'friend' dashed along the platform, but too late; he shrugged and waved to me. I raised my hand in acknowledgement.

I woke as usual approaching Harpenden, and stood up to stretch myself. I really did feel dizzy. Must take it easy when the budget was finished; take a good holiday, after my hospital visit. I couldn't resist counting my ten pieces of paper again. Then I noticed a newspaper on the opposite seat. Surely it hadn't been there before? It was open on an inside page, and a modest headline stood out:

BODY DISCOVERED BY CLEANER ON TRAIN AT BEDFORD
In an exclusive interview, the cleaner told our reporter, 'I had just cleared up some bits of paper from the floor into my trolley and found the body between the seats …'

The pain shot through my chest. I couldn't breathe, like a band had been suddenly tightened round me. I dropped my betting slips and staggered to the next seat …

THE DIVING PLATFORM

Patrick Marlowe

I USED TO COME HERE with my grandparents. Every summer, Mummy and Daddy would drive me from London, have lunch (Grandma and Grandpa were Daddy's Mummy and Daddy) and then leave me for a week. Those weeks were always the happiest of my life, filled with fun and laughter, sunshine and love. Unfortunately, there weren't many of them, as I lost Grandma and Grandpa when I was still quite a little boy. Anyway, every year, on my last day, the three of us would climb into Grandpa's car, and he'd drive us all here. We'd stay all day. Sometimes Grandma and Grandpa would come down on to the beach, but when I got a bit older, they'd sit on one of the benches halfway down the path, Grandma with her knitting and Grandpa with his newspaper, and they'd keep an eye on me while I built sandcastles or paddled in the shallows, sunburnt and carefree. The only rule was that I had to stay where they could see me.

Grandpa liked that bench the best, because it was surrounded by rosebushes and he loved roses and used to say that the only good reason for being famous was that someone might name a rose after you. I wanted to name a rose after him, even though he wasn't famous, and I was going to do it, when I got bigger, for his birthday, but I never got the chance.

I was never lonely on those days, because there were always other children to play with, and other children wanted to play with me because Grandma and Grandpa always bought me a brand-new bucket and spade or a beach ball.

Some of the children had beach huts and once I was invited in to one and it was lovely in there and they were a nice family, and I decided there and then that I would have a beach hut when I was big, and I never did that either. I remember that when I was in there, all hell was suddenly let loose outside. There was shouting and all sorts of commotion which was strange because usually the only raised voices you ever heard were laughing. We peeped outside and it was Grandma and Grandpa with some people I'd never seen before and they were all shouting my name, and I heard Grandma saying 'He's blonde and about this high and wearing red trunks.' I didn't half get a rocket from Grandpa when I came out because when I'd been in the beach hut they couldn't see me and they didn't know where I was and they'd got really frightened and

I cried and cried because I didn't understand why Grandpa was so angry rather than being happy to see me. He'd never been cross with me before and I knew I'd upset Grandma and after that we went straight to their car and drove back to their house in silence, and I never set foot inside a beach hut again.

We did come back here for the next few years, and as I got bigger I was allowed to go a bit further into the sea, as long as they could see me. In those days, there was a diving platform floating what seemed an awfully long way out with a ladder going down into the sea. Grandpa told me that it was anchored to the sea bed so that sunbathers didn't fall asleep and wake up in France, which he said was a fate worse than death. You had a great view of the platform from Grandma and Grandpa's bench. It was always full of bigger children clambering on and jumping off and I longed to go out there to clamber on and jump off, but Grandma and Grandpa said it was too far out and that I wasn't a strong enough swimmer and maybe I could do it when I was bigger. I used to watch the other children enviously and wonder what bigger meant, and how you'd know when you arrived at it, or whether bigger was just an excuse that grown-ups used to stop you doing things they were frightened of.

One year, a couple of years after the beach hut, when I was bigger, but still not by enough, I went out to the diving platform without permission. I'd been playing quite happily on my own, when a boy I'd never seen before came along and smashed up the sandcastle I was building. It was a very big and detailed castle, with crenellated battlements, and gargoyles made from shells, and a driftwood drawbridge, and topped off with a new flag Grandma had bought me. I'd worked really hard on it, and made up stories in my head about the knights and fine ladies who lived in it, and I couldn't wait to show it to Grandma and Grandpa. He came up and stood looking at it, for a moment. 'That must have taken for ever,' he said. I nodded and he said, 'Loser,' and kicked it all in. Then he pushed me over, and ran away laughing. He ran towards my brand-new beach ball which had blown along the beach a bit, and he picked it up and I chased after him and told him to give it back and he called me a name and said I'd have to get it off him, but he was holding it too high, and I couldn't reach, and then he pushed me over again and picked up a piece of shell and popped my brand-new beach ball and threw it at me, and walked away laughing.

Trying not to cry (not in front of him, anyway), I went back up to the bench among the roses to ask Grandma and Grandpa if I could have an ice cream (which was always an expedition because they weren't allowed to sell them on the beach and you had to go back into town). They'd both nodded off in the sunshine, and it didn't seem right to wake them up just for an ice cream. As they were asleep, they weren't living up to their part of the bargain, so I decided there and then to swim out to the diving platform. I didn't want to be on the beach with the horrible boy anyway, and there was nothing else to do.

It was exciting going out there, exciting and frightening, and as I got closer, I started to wish I hadn't because the sea was lapping against my chin and every wave carried my feet off the bottom and I'd drift away to the side a little and I was getting tired and worried about how I'd get back and about how upset Grandma and Grandpa would be if they woke up while I was still out there and then suddenly I was holding on to the ladder. I heaved myself up and lay on the deck. It was made of wood, quite splintery and rough and lovely and warm. There was no one else on it, so I lay down for a while with my eyes shut, feeling the breeze and gently bobbing up and down with the sea, as if we were both breathing together. Every so often a shout of laughter would be blown to me from the beach, and I could feel the little hairs on my legs straightening up one by one as the sun dried them. I felt more tingling and alive at that moment than I ever had before. The fact that I wasn't supposed to be there made it even better. I'd finally arrived at bigger, and I knew that when I told Grandma and Grandpa they'd understand.

Suddenly there was a terrible pain in my side. I opened my eyes, and there was the nasty boy, kicking me.

'This is my castle,' he said. 'You've got to get off.'

He kicked me again. I started to get up.

'It's not a castle,' I said. 'It's a diving platform and everyone's allowed to be here.'

'You're not,' he said, and pushed me really hard.

'You're a bully,' I said, trying my hardest not to cry.

'You're a girl,' he said.

'I'm not,' I said.

'You cry like one,' he said, and pushed me again. 'Are you going to get off, or do I have to make you?'

'I hate you,' I said.

'Good,' he said. 'I hate all girls.'

'I'm not a girl!'

All the time he was moving closer to me. I backed away, trying to stay out of reach. Suddenly, he lurched forwards, and shoved me with all his might, and I was flying through the air.

That was the last year coming here with Grandma and Grandpa. I lost them when I was still young, but the memory of those summer days is still so vivid, and the place still exerts a strange pull. There are new grandparents looking after new grandchildren, sitting on the bench among the roses. The beach huts have new people in them, sometimes the children I played with, grown up. In town there are new shops, but you still can't get an ice cream on the beach. The diving platform's gone. It went in my last year because some kid went out there and must have fallen off and he was found ten days later two miles up the coast with a big lump out of his head. When you're here all the time, you don't notice the changes so much. It's like when you're a child and someone who hasn't seen you for a year says, 'Haven't you grown?', when people who see you every day don't notice.

It's still mostly a place for people at either end of their lives. People in their middle years, who want more sophisticated pleasures don't come here until they've got children or old people of their own, and that's the way we like it.

Each summer I come back. I can't help it. Something brings me back here; the forlorn hope of recapturing the past, perhaps. I go about my business, no one notices me, and I don't bother them. I don't make friends easily, and sometimes I'm very lonely. I still felt like the little boy who came here with his grandparents and looked for other children to play with.

And this year, I got my wish. He came back. I knew he would. Everyone does eventually, and I'd been waiting for him. Such a long time. He'd changed, of course. A middle-aged man now, with a wife and children of his own. I knew him straight away, and even if I hadn't, his son looked the dead spit of him all those years ago. I sat down beside them on the beach. They didn't notice me, but I could hear them.

'Why didn't you want to come here, Daddy?' said the boy. He seemed a very sensitive, sweet-natured little boy, not like his father had been. I would have loved to have played with him.

'It's not that I didn't want to. I just don't remember this place as fondly as Mummy does, that's all. She wanted to come back and have an all our yesterdays, so here we are.'

'You might have played here with Mummy when you were children, never knowing that you'd end up married.'

'Yes, I suppose it's possible. But I played with all sorts of children. Mostly boys.'

He looked out to sea, lost in thought. Suddenly, I saw him start.

'Good God,' he said. 'I thought they'd got rid of that thing years ago.'

'What thing, Daddy?'

'Out there. It's a diving platform. Can't believe I hadn't noticed it before.'

'Can we go out there, Daddy?'

'Absolutely not. Far too dangerous. Those things are an accident waiting to happen.'

'Please.'

'No. It's too far out and you're not a strong enough swimmer. Now stop going on about it. Your mother will be back with the ice creams before you know it.'

As the afternoon wore on, he kept looking anxiously out to sea, but eventually, he lay down and nodded off, as I knew he would.

His son was down on the beach, building a sandcastle. I walked across the warm, wet sand and tapped him on the shoulder. He looked up at me and smiled. It was the most lovely smile. I bent down and whispered in his ear. He looked over at his sleeping father and nodded. He stood up, and hand in hand we walked down to the sea.

We had such fun on the diving platform, feeling the sun beating down on the deck as we rose and fell with the waves. Suddenly, we heard a shout, and we could see his father swimming towards us. He climbed up the ladder and stood there dripping and breathing heavily.

'What the hell do you think you're playing at?' he shouted. 'I told you you weren't allowed to come out here. How dare you? Come here this instant.'

At that moment, he saw me. I smiled. He frowned at me, as if he was remembering something. And then I saw all the colour drain from his face.

'Right now. Don't stand there gaping at me!' he screamed. 'This minute, or I'll give you a bloody good hiding.'

I could see that he was frightening his son, who was cowering and backing slowly away.

'I said, now!' He started advancing on the boy. I knew what was going to happen, but there was nothing I could do to stop it.

When he came back to the surface, I stretched out my hand and helped him up the ladder. We sat side by side on the warm deck, holding hands. Somehow the platform had come adrift and we were slowly floating away from the shore. His father was frantically swimming backwards and forwards and every so often we could hear him desperately crying out his son's name.

We turned to each other and smiled.

I'll come back again next summer. But now, I'll never be lonely again.

If you enjoyed this book...
...then you'll love Saga Magazine

It's the home of great writing, fascinating interviews, peerless advice on a huge range of subjects from finance, health and gardening to technology, food and travel - all with lively, intelligent readers over 50 in mind

Join our family of discerning readers who have made Saga Magazine the bestselling title in the UK. Subscribe now – it's just £19.99 for a year!

It's what you read when you grow up